THE SPACE PIONEERS

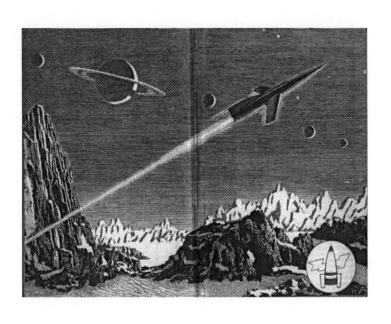

CAREY ROCKWELL

THE SPACE PIONEERS

LOUIS GLANZMAN
Illustrator

WILLY LEY
Technical Adviser

BIBLIOBAZAAR

THE SPACE PIONEERS

CONTENTS

ILLUSTRATIONS

CHAPTER 1

"Go on, Astro," shouted the young Space Cadet. "Boot that screwy ball with everything you've got!"

The three cadets of the *Polaris* unit raced down the Academy field toward the mercuryball, a plastic sphere with a vial of mercury inside. At the opposite end of the field, three members of the *Arcturus* unit ran headlong in a desperate effort to reach the ball first.

Astro, the giant Space Cadet from Venus, charged toward the ball like a blazing rocket, while his two unit mates flanked him, ready to block out their opponents and give Astro a clear shot at the ball.

On the left wing, Tom Corbett, curly-haired and snub-nosed, ran lightly down the field, while on the opposite wing, Roger Manning, his blond hair cut crew style, kept pace with him easily. The two teams closed. Roger threw a perfect block on his opposing wingman and the two boys went down in a heap. Tom side-stepped the *Arcturus* cadet on his side and sent him sprawling to the ground. He quickly cut across the field and threw his body headlong at the last remaining member of the opposition. Astro was free to kick the ball perfectly for a fifty-yard goal.

Jogging back toward their own goal line, the three *Polaris* cadets congratulated each other. Astro's kick had tied the score, two-all.

"That was some feint you pulled on Richards, Tom," said Roger. "You sucked him in beautifully. I thought he was going to tear up the field with his nose!"

Tom grinned. Compliments from Roger were few and far between.

Astro clapped his hands together and roared, "All right, fellas, let's see if we can't take these space bums again! Another shot at the goal—that's all I need!"

Lining up at the end of the field again, the cadets kept their eyes on the cadet referee on the side lines. They saw him hold up his hand and then drop it suddenly. Once again the teams raced toward the ball in the middle of the field. When they met, Roger tried to duplicate Tom's feat and feint his opponent, but the other cadet was ready for the maneuver and stopped dead in his tracks. Roger was forced to break stride just long enough for the *Arcturus* cadet to dump him to the ground and then race for Astro. Tom, covering Astro on the left wing, saw the cadet sweeping in and lunged in a desperate attempt to stop him. But he missed, leaving Astro unprotected against the three members of the *Arcturus* unit. With his defense gone, Astro kicked at the ball frantically but just grazed the side of it. The mercury inside the ball began to play its role in the game, and as though it had a brain of its own, the ball spun, stopped, bounced, and spiraled in every direction, with the cadets kicking, lunging, and scrambling for a clean shot. Finally Astro reached the tumbling sphere and booted it away from the group. There was a roar of laughter from the *Arcturus* unit and a low groan from Tom and Roger. Astro saw that he had kicked the ball over his own goal line.

"Why, you clobber-headed Venusian hick!" yelled Roger. "Can't you tell the difference between our goal and theirs?"

Astro grinned sheepishly as the three jogged back to their own goal to line up once more.

"Lay off, Roger," said Tom. "How come you didn't get Richards on that play?"

"I slipped," replied the blond cadet.

"Yeah, you slipped all right," growled Astro good-naturedly, "with a great big assist from Richards."

"Ah, go blast your jets," grumbled Roger. "Come on! Let's show those space crawlers what this game is all about!"

But before the cadet referee could drop his hand, a powerful, low-slung jet car, its exhaust howling, pulled to a screeching stop at the edge of the field and a scarlet-clad enlisted Solar Guardsman jumped out and spoke to him. Sensing that it was something important, the two teams jogged over to surround the messenger.

"What's up, Joe?" asked Roger.

The enlisted spaceman, an Earthworm cadet who had washed out of the Academy but had re-enlisted in the Solar

Guard, smiled. "Orders for the *Polaris* unit," he said, "from Captain Strong."

"What about?" asked Roger.

"Report on the double for new assignments," replied the guardsman.

"Yeeeeooooow!" Astro roared in jubilation. "At last we can get out of here. I've been doing so blamed much classroom work, I've forgotten what space looks like."

"Know where we're going, Joe?" asked Tom.

"Uh-uh." Joe shook his head. He turned away, then stopped, and called back, "Want a lift back to the Tower?"

Before Tom could answer, Richards, the captain of the *Arcturus* unit spoke up. "How about finishing the game, Tom? It's been so long since we've had such good competition we hate to lose you. Come on. Only a few more minutes."

Tom hesitated. It had been a long time since the two units had played together, but orders were orders. He looked at Roger and Astro. "Well, what about it?"

"Sure," said Roger. "We'll wipe up these space jokers in nothing flat! Come on!"

There was a mock yell of anger from the *Arcturus* unit and the two teams raced back to their starting positions. In the remaining minutes of play, the cadets played hard and rough. First one team would score and then the other. A sizable crowd of cadets had gathered to watch the game and cheered lustily as the players tore up and down the field. Finally, when both teams were nearly exhausted, the game was over and the score was eight to seven in favor of the *Polaris* unit. Roger had made the final point after Tony Richards had left the game with a badly bruised hip. A substitute called in from the bystanders, an Earthworm cadet, had eagerly joined the *Arcturus* team for the last minutes of play but had been hopelessly outclassed by the teamwork of the *Polaris* unit.

Promising a return match soon, Roger, Tom, and Astro hurried to their lockers, showered, and dressed in their senior cadet uniforms of vivid blue, then raced to the nearest slidewalk to head toward the main group of buildings that made up Space Academy.

Whisked along on the moving belt of plastic that formed the principle method of transportation in and around the Academy grounds, Tom turned to his unit mates. "What do you think it'll be?" he asked.

"You mean the assignment?" asked Roger, answering his own question in the next breath. "I don't know. But anything to get out of here. I've been on Earth so long that I'm getting gravity-itis!"

Tom smiled. "It'll sure be nice to get up in the wide, high, and deep again," he said, glancing up at the cloudless sky.

"Say it again, spaceman," breathed Astro. "One more lesson on the differential potential between chemical-burning rocket fuels and reactant energy and I'll blast off without a spaceship!"

Roger and Tom laughed. They both sympathized with the big cadet's inability to cope with the theory of atomic energy and fuel conservation in spaceships. In charge of the power deck on the *Polaris*, Astro earlier had gained firsthand experience in commercial rocket ships as an able spaceman and later had been accepted in the Academy for cadet training. The son of colonists on Venus, the misty planet, his formal education was limited, and though he had no equal while on the power deck of a rocket ship, in theory and classroom study he had to depend on Roger and Tom to help him get passing grades.

The slidewalk moved smoothly and easily toward the gleaming Tower of Galileo, the largest and most imposing of the structures of Space Academy. Made entirely of clear crystal mined on Titan, satellite of Saturn, the Tower rose over the smaller buildings like a giant shimmering jewel. Housing the administration offices of the Solar Guard and the Space Academy staff, it also contained Galaxy Hall, the museum of space, which attracted thousands of visitors from every part of the Solar Alliance.

Tom Corbett, his eyes caressing the magnificent gleaming Tower, remembered the first time he had seen it. While it hadn't been so long in months or years since becoming a Space Cadet, it seemed as though he had been at the Academy all of his life and that it was his home. In the struggle to develop into a well-knit dependable rocket team, composed of an astrogator, power-deck cadet, and a command cadet, Tom had assumed the leadership of the unit, and the relationship between Astro,

Roger Manning, and himself had ripened until they were more like brothers than three young men who had grown up millions of miles apart.

As they rode toward the Tower, the three cadets could see the green-clad first-year Earthworms getting their first taste of cadet life—hours of close-order formations and drills. The nearer they came to the Tower, the more intense and colorful became the activity as the crisscrossing slidewalks carried enlisted guardsmen in their red uniforms, and the officers of the Solar Guard in magnificent black and gold, across the quadrangle to the various dormitories, laboratories, lecture rooms, mess halls, and research rooms. Space Academy was a beehive of activity, with the education of thousands of cadets and the operational mechanics of the Solar Guard going on incessantly, day and night, never stopping in its avowed task of defending the liberties of the planets, safeguarding the freedom of space, and upholding the cause of peace throughout the universe.

As their slidewalk glided over the quadrangle, Roger suddenly turned to his unit mates. "Think we might get assigned to that radar project they're setting up on the Moon?" he asked. "I have a few ideas—"

Tom laughed. "He can't wait until he gets his hands on that new scanner Dr. Dale just finished, Astro," he said with a wink.

The big Venusian snorted. "Can you imagine the ego of that guy? Dr. Dale spends almost a year building that thing, with the help of the leading electronic scientists in the Alliance, and *he* can't wait to *tell* them about a few of *his* ideas!"

"I didn't mean that," complained Roger. "All I said was—"

"You don't have to say a word, hot-shot," interrupted Astro. "I can read your thoughts as though they were flashed on a stereo screen!"

"Oh, yeah!" growled Roger. "You should be that telepathic for your exams. Why didn't you read my thoughts when I beat my brains out trying to explain that thrust problem the other night?" He turned to Tom, shrugging his shoulders in mock despair. "Honestly, Tom, if I didn't know that he was the best power jockey in the Academy, I'd say he was the dumbest thing to leave Venus, *including* the dinosaurs in the Academy Zoo!"

With a hamlike hand Astro suddenly grabbed for Roger's neck, but the wiry cadet dashed along the slidewalk out of reach and the big Venusian rumbled after him. Tom roared with laughter.

As he started to follow his unit mates, one of the passengers on the slidewalk grabbed Tom by the arm and he turned to see Mike McKenny, Chief Warrant Officer in the enlisted Solar Guard and the first instructor the *Polaris* unit had met on their arrival at the Academy.

"Corbett!" demanded McKenny. "Are those two space crawlers still acting like monkeys out of their cages?"

Tom laughed and shook hands with the elderly spaceman. "Yes, sir," he said. "But you could hardly call Astro a monkey!"

"More along the lines of a Venusian gorilla, if you ask me!" snorted McKenny. The short, squat spaceman's eyes twinkled. "I've been hearing some mighty fine things about you three space bongos, Tommy. It's a wonder the Solar Guard didn't give you a unit citation for aiding in the capture of Coxine, the pirate!"

"Thanks, Mike. Coming from you that compliment really means something!"

"Just be sure you keep those two space lunatics in their proper cages," said Mike, indicating Roger and Astro, who at the moment were racing back and forth along the slidewalk bumping passengers left and right, "and you'll all be heroes someday."

"Yes, sir," said Tom. He glanced up, and noticing that he was in front of the Tower building, hopped to the walkway, waving a cheery good-by to Mike. "Blast over to our mess and have dinner with us some night, Mike!" he yelled to the departing figure.

"And interrupt the happiest hours in Astro's life?" bawled Mike. "No thank you!"

Tom laughed and turned to the huge open doorway of the Tower where Roger and Astro waited for him impatiently. In a few moments the three were being carried to the upper floors of the crystal structure by a spiraling band of moving plastic that stretched from the top of the Tower to the many floors below surface level. Tom glanced at his wrist chronograph as they stepped off the slidestairs and headed for Captain Strong's quarters.

"We're about twenty minutes late," he said to Roger and Astro. "Hope Captain Strong's in good spirits!"

"If he isn't," said Roger, "we can—"

"Don't say it," protested Astro. "I only just finished working off my last bunch of galley demerits."

They stopped in front of a door, straightened their uniforms, and then slid the door to one side and stepped smartly into the room. They came to rigid attention before a massive desk, flanked by two wall windows of clear sheet crystal reaching from ceiling to floor. Standing at the window, Captain Steve Strong, *Polaris* unit cadet supervisor, his broad shoulders stretching under his black-and-gold uniform, turned to face them, his features set in grim lines of trouble.

"Polaris unit reporting for orders, sir," said Tom. The three cadets saluted crisply.

Strong snapped a return salute and walked to the front of his desk. "Getting pretty big for your britches, aren't you?" he growled. "I've been watching you from this window. I saw the messenger deliver my orders to you, and then, I saw you return to your game and finish it, apparently deciding that the business of the Solar Guard can wait!"

"But, sir—" Roger started to say.

"Close your exhaust, Manning!" snapped Strong. "I'm doing the talking!"

"Yes, sir," stammered the blond-haired cadet.

"Well, Cadets," asked Strong in a silken voice, "if I sent you to Commander Walters' office *on the double*, do you think I could trust you to get there on the *double?*"

"Oh, yes, sir," replied Tom. *"Yes, sir!"* The other two boys nodded violently.

"Then blast out of here and report to Commander Walters for your assignments. Tell him I'll be there in a few minutes."

"Yes, sir!" said Tom, and the three cadets saluted sharply.

"Unit—" bawled Strong, *"dis*—missed!"

Outside in the hall once more, the three cadets wiped their faces.

"Captain Strong definitely was not in a good mood!" commented Roger.

"I've never seen him so angry!" said Tom. "Wonder why."

"Think it might be something to do with our assignments?" asked Astro.

"Never can tell, Astro," said Tom. "And there's only one way to find out. That's to get to Commander Walters' office on the double!"

Without another word the cadets hurried to the slidestairs, each of them hungry for excitement. Already having participated in three outstanding adventures, the cadet members of the *Polaris* unit were eager to begin a fourth.

CHAPTER 2

"There's no doubt that the success or failure of this project will influence the thinking of the Solar Alliance with regard to further expansion, Governor Hardy," said Commander Walters to the man sitting stiffly in front of him. "And my congratulations on your appointment to head the expedition."

A tall, lean man with iron-gray hair, the commander of Space Academy, sat behind his desk, back ramrod straight in his black-and-gold senior officer's uniform, and casually toyed with a paper cutter on his desk as he spoke to Christopher Hardy, a short, thin man with a balding head and sharp features.

"Thank you, Commander," replied Hardy, in a thin, reedy voice. "It's a great honor and I certainly don't foresee anything that can prevent the expedition from being a complete success. We have the best equipment and, I hope, we'll have the finest men."

The soft chime of a muted bell interrupted Walters as he was about to reply. He opened the switch to the interoffice teleceiver behind his desk, then watched the image of his aide appear on the teleceiver screen.

"What is it, Bill?" asked Walters.

"*Polaris* unit reporting for orders, sir," replied the enlisted guardsman. "Cadets Corbett, Manning, and Astro."

"Very well, send them in," said Walters. Switching off the teleceiver, he turned back to Governor Hardy. "Ever hear of the *Polaris* unit, sir?" he asked.

Hardy paused, rubbing his chin before answering. "No, can't say that I have." He smiled. "From the look on your face, I see I should know about them, though."

Walters smiled back. "I'll just say this about them. Of all the cadet units trained here at the Academy in the last twenty years, these three lads are just about perfection. Just the material you'll need on your initial operation."

Governor Hardy raised his hand in mock protest. "Please! No brain trusts!"

"Well, they have the brains all right." Walters laughed. "But they have something else, an instinctive ability to do the right thing at the right time and that indefinable something that makes them true men of space, rather than ordinary ground hogs simply transplanted into space."

As the commander spoke, the massive door to his office rolled back and Tom, Roger, and Astro stepped in briskly, coming to stiff attention in front of the desk.

"*Polaris* unit reporting for duty, sir," said Tom. "Cadets Corbett, Manning, and Astro."

"At ease," said Walters.

The three boys relaxed and glanced quickly at the governor who had watched their entrance with interest. Walters came around in front of the desk and gestured toward Hardy.

"Boys, I want you to meet Governor Hardy."

The three cadets nodded respectfully. They knew all about the governor's achievements in establishing the first colony on Ganymede, and his success with the first exploratory expedition to outer space.

"Sit down, boys," said Walters, indicating a near-by couch. "Governor Hardy will explain things from here on in. Where is Captain Strong?"

"He said he'd be along in a few moments, sir," replied Roger.

"Well," said Walters, turning to Hardy, "no sense in beginning without Steve. Only have to repeat yourself." He turned to Astro but not before he saw a grimace of annoyance cloud the governor's face. "How are you making out with your classroom studies, Astro?"

"Uh—ah—" stammered the giant Venusian, "I'm doing all right, sir," he managed finally.

Walters suppressed a smile and turned to Hardy.

"One of the most important aspects of our training methods here at the Academy, Governor," began Walters, returning to his desk, "is for the cadet to learn to depend on his unit mates. Take Astro, for instance."

The two men glanced at the big cadet who shuffled his feet in embarrassment at being the center of attention.

"Astro," continued Walters, "is rather shaky in the field of theory and abstract-scientific concepts. Yet he is capable of handling practically any situation on the power deck of a spaceship. He literally thinks with his hands."

"Most commendable," commented Hardy dryly. "But I should think it would be difficult if he ever came face to face with a situation where his hands were bound." There was the lightest touch of sarcasm in his voice.

"I assure you, Governor," said Walters, "that wouldn't stop him either. But my point is this: Since a cadet unit is assembled only after careful study of their individual psychograph personality charts and is passed and failed as a unit, even though a boy like Cadet Astro might make a failing grade, his unit mates, Cadets Manning and Corbett, can pull him through by making higher passing marks. You see, an average is taken for all three and they pass or fail as a unit."

"Then they are forced, more or less, to depend on each other?" asked Hardy.

"Yes. In the beginning of their training. Later on, the cadets learn for themselves that it is better for all of them to work together."

Once again the bell in back of Walters' desk chimed and he turned to speak on the teleceiver to his aide.

"Captain Strong is here, sir," repeated the enlisted man.

"Send him right in," said Walters. Seconds later the door slid back and Steve Strong entered and saluted.

After the introductions were completed and the Solar Guard captain had taken a seat with his cadet unit, Commander Walters immediately launched into the purpose of the meeting.

"Steve," he began, "Governor Hardy here has been appointed by the Solar Council to head one of the most important projects yet attempted by the Alliance."

The cadets edged to the front of the couch and listened intently for what the commander was about to say.

"But perhaps I had better let the governor tell you about it himself," concluded Walters abruptly and settled back in his chair.

Captain Strong and the cadets swung around to face the governor, who rose and looked at each of them steadily before speaking.

"Commander Walters stressed the fact that this was an important project," he said finally. "No one can say how important it will be for the future. It might mean the beginning of an entirely new era in the development of mankind." He paused again. "The Solar Alliance has decided to establish a new colony," he announced. "The first colony of its kind outside the solar system in deep space!"

"A star colony!" gasped Strong.

The cadets muttered excitedly among themselves.

"The decision," continued the governor, "has been made only after much debate in the Solar Council Chamber. There have been many arguments pro and con. A week ago a secret vote was taken, and the project was approved. We are going to establish a Solar Alliance colony on a newly discovered satellite in orbit around the sun star Wolf 359, a satellite that has been named Roald."

"Wolf 359!" exclaimed Roger. "That's more than thirteen light years away—" He was stopped by Tom's hand clamped across his mouth.

Governor Hardy looked at Roger and smiled. "Yes, Wolf 359 is pretty far away, especially for a colony. But preliminary expeditions have investigated and found the satellite suitable for habitation, with fertile soil and an atmosphere similar to our own. With the aid of a few atmosphere booster stations, it should be as easy for a colonist to live there as he would on Venus—or any tropical planet."

"Where are you going to get the colonists, sir?" asked Strong.

Hardy began to pace back and forth in front of Walters' desk, waving his hands as he warmed up to his subject. "Tonight, on a special combined audioceiver and televiser broadcast to all parts of the Solar Alliance, the president of the Solar Council will ask for volunteers—men who will take man's first step through deep space to the stars. It is a step, which, in the thousands of years ahead, will eventually lead to a civilization of Earthmen throughout all space!"

Tom, Roger, and Astro sat in silent awe as they listened to the plans for man to reach toward the stars. Spacemen by nature and adventurers in spirit, they were united in the belief that some day Earthmen would set foot on all the stars and never stop until they had seen the last sun, the last world, the last unexplored corner of the cosmos.

"The colonists," continued Hardy, "will come from all over the system. One thousand of them—the strongest and sturdiest men out of the billions that inhabit the planets around us; one thousand, to live on Roald for a period of seven years."

Tom, his eyes bright, asked, "Won't everybody want to go, sir?"

Walters and Hardy smiled. "We expect a rush, Corbett," answered Walters. "You three and Captain Strong have been selected to aid in screening the applicants."

"Will there be any special tests, sir?" asked Strong. "I have to agree with Corbett that just about everyone will want to go."

"Yes, Strong," said Hardy. "Everyone *will* want to go. In fact, we estimate that there will be literally millions of applicants!"

Roger emitted a long, low whistle. "It'll take years to screen all of them, sir."

Hardy smiled. "Not really, Manning. The psychographs will eliminate the hundreds of thousands of misfits, the men who will want to go for selfish reasons, who are running away from the past, or are dissatisfied with their lack of success in life and embittered because of failure. We can expect many criminal types. Those will be eliminated easily. We have set a specific quota from each of the satellites, planets, and asteroid colonies. I have already established the stations for the preliminary screening. We will screen the remainder until we have the required thousand."

"What will our part be, sir?" asked Tom.

"Once each applicant has been approved by the psychographs, his background will be thoroughly investigated. We may find criminal types who show the blackest of careers, but who would turn over a new leaf if given the chance and prove to be more valuable than men with the best of backgrounds who merely want to get away from it all. We don't want that kind of colonist. We want people who have faith in the project; people who are not afraid of work and hardships. Your screening job will be simple. Each of you has a special talent which Commander Walters feels is outstanding. Corbett in leadership, administration, and command;

Manning in electronics; Astro in atomic power and propulsion. You will talk to the applicants and give them simple tests. An important point in any applicant's favor will be his ability to improvise and handle three, four, or five jobs, where a less imaginative person would do but one. Talk to them, sound them out, and then write your report. Captain Strong will review your opinions and make recommendations to me. I will finally approve or disapprove the applications."

"Will this cost the applicants anything, sir?" asked Roger. "For instance, will the rich applicants have a better chance than the poor?"

Hardy's face turned grim. "Only the people that fit our standards will be allowed to go, Manning. Regardless."

"Yes, sir," said Roger.

"The Solar Alliance," continued Hardy, "has established a fund for this project. Each applicant will be lent as much in material as he needs to establish himself on Roald. If he operates an exchange, for instance, selling clothes, equipment, or food, then the size of his exchange will determine the size of the loan. He will repay the Solar Alliance by returning one-fourth of his profits over a period of seven years. Each colonist will be required to remain on the satellite for that seven-year period. After that, should he leave, he would be required to sell all his rights and property on Roald."

"And the farmers, sir," asked Tom, "and all the rest. Will they all be treated the same way?"

"Exactly the same, according to their individual abilities. Of course we wouldn't take a man who had been a shoemaker and advance him the capital to become a farmer."

"Will the quota of one thousand colonists include women and children?" asked Astro.

"No, but allowances have been made for them. One thousand colonists means one thousand men *who can produce*. However, a man may take his family," Hardy went on, adding, "providing, of course, that he doesn't mean twenty-three children, aunts, uncles, and so forth."

The three cadets looked at each other dumfounded. The very idea of the project was staggering, and as Strong, Hardy, and Commander Walters began to discuss the details of the screening system, they turned to each other excitedly.

"This is the greatest thing that's happened since Jon Builker made his trip into deep space!" whispered Tom.

"Yeah," nodded Astro, "but I'm scared."

"About what?" asked Roger.

"Having the responsibility of saying No to a feller that wants to go."

The big cadet seemed to be worried and Tom attempted to explain what the job would really be.

"It's not a question of saying an outright No," said Tom. "You just ask the applicant about his experience with motors and reactors to see if he really knows his stuff."

Astro seemed to accept Tom's explanation, but he still seemed concerned as they all turned to Commander Walters, who had finished the discussion around the desk and was giving Captain Strong his orders.

"You and the cadets, along with Governor Hardy, will blast off tonight and go to Venusport for the first screenings." He faced the cadets. "You three boys have a tremendous responsibility. In many cases your decisions might mean the difference between success or failure in this mission. See that you make good decisions, and when you've made them, stick by them. You will be under the direct supervision of Captain Strong and Governor Hardy. This is quite different from your previous assignments, but I have faith in you. See that you handle yourselves like spacemen."

The three cadets saluted sharply, and after shaking hands with their commander, left the room.

Later that evening, their gear packed, the three members of the *Polaris* unit were checked out of the Academy by the dormitory officer and were soon being whisked along on a slidewalk to the Academy spaceport. As they neared the spacious concrete field, where the mighty fleet of the Solar Guard was based, they could see the rows of rocket cruisers, destroyers, scouts, and various types of merchant space craft, and in the center, on a launching platform, the silhouette of the rocket cruiser *Polaris* stood out boldly against the pale evening sky. Resting on her directional fins, her nose pointed skyward, her gleaming hull reflecting the last rays of the setting sun, the ship was a powerful projectile ready to blast off for distant worlds.

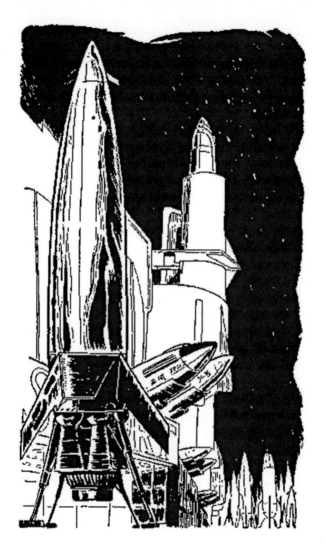

Her nose pointed skyward, the Polaris *was ready to blast off*

Reaching the *Polaris*, the three cadets scrambled through the air lock into the spaceship and prepared for blast-off.

On the control deck, Tom began the involved check of the control panel. One by one, he tested the dials, gauges, and indicators on the instrument panel that was the brains of the mighty ship.

On the radar bridge, above the control deck, Roger adjusted the sights of the precious astrogation prism and took a checking sight on the Pole Star to make sure the instrument was in true alignment. Then turning to the radar scanner, the all-seeing eye of the ship, he began a slow, deliberate tracking of each circuit in the maze of wiring.

And below on the power deck, Astro, stripped to the waist, a leather belt filled with the rocketman's wrenches and tools slung around his hips, tuned up the mighty atomic engines. He took longer than usual, making sure the lead baffling around the reactor units and the reaction chamber was secure, before firing the initial mass.

Finally Tom's voice crackled over the intercom, "Control deck to all stations. Check in!"

"Radar bridge, aye!" came Roger's reply. "Ready for blast-off!"

"Power deck, aye!" said Astro, his booming voice echoing through the ship. "Ready for blast-off!"

"Control deck, ready for blast-off," said Tom, and then turned to the logbook and jotted down the time in the ship's journal. The astral chronometer over the control board read exactly 1350 hours.

Fifteen minutes later Captain Strong and Governor Hardy climbed aboard and Tom received the order to raise ship.

The young curly-haired cadet turned to the control board and flipped on the teleceiver. "Rocket cruiser *Polaris* to spaceport control tower," he called. "Request blast-off orbit and clearance!"

The traffic-control officer in the spaceport tower answered immediately. "Control tower to *Polaris*. You are cleared for blast-off at 1405 hours, orbital tangent 867."

Tom repeated the instructions and turned to the intercom and began snapping out orders. "Power deck, energize the cooling pumps!"

"Power deck, aye!" replied Astro. The slow whine of the powerful pumps began to scream through the ship. Tom watched the pressure indicator and when it reached the blast-off mark called to Roger for clearance.

"All clear, forward and up!" declared Roger.

"Feed reactant at D-9 rate!" ordered Tom. And far below on the power deck, Astro began to feed the reactant energy into the firing chambers.

Hardy looked at Strong and nodded in appreciation of the cadets' smooth efficient work. They strapped themselves into acceleration cushions and watched the red second hand of the astral chronometer sweep around, and then heard Tom counting off the seconds.

"Blast off—" bawled Tom, "minus five—four—three—two—one—*zeroooo!*"

The giant ship lurched off the blast-off platform a few feet, the exhaust of the powerful rockets deflected against the concrete surface. Then, poised delicately on the roaring rockets, the mighty ship picked up speed and began to accelerate through the atmosphere.

Pushed deep in his acceleration chair in front of the control board, unable to move because of the tremendous pressure against his body, Tom Corbett thought about his new adventure. And as the ship hurtled into the black velvet depths of space, he wondered what the future held for him as he and his unit mates began a new adventure among the stars.

CHAPTER 3

"Control deck to power deck, check in!" Tom's voice crackled over the power-deck loud-speaker and Astro snapped to quick attention.

"Power deck, aye!" replied the giant Venusian into the intercom microphone. "What's up?"

"Stand by for course change," said Tom. "Roger's picked up a meteor on the radar scanner and—"

"Here's the course change," Roger's voice broke in over the intercom. "Three degrees up on the plane of the ecliptic and five degrees starboard!"

"Get that, Astro?" snapped Tom. "Stand by for one-quarter burst on steering rockets!"

"One-quarter—right!" acknowledged the power-deck cadet and turned to the massive panel that controlled the rockets.

On the control deck Tom Corbett continued talking to Roger. "Relay the pickup to the control-deck scanner, Roger," he ordered. "Let me take a look at that thing."

In a moment the thin sweeping white line on the control-deck scanner swept around the green surface of the screen, picking out the blip that marked the meteor. Tom watched it for a moment and then barked into the intercom, "Stand by to execute change course!"

He watched the meteor a few more seconds, making sure the course change would take them out of its path, and then gave the command. "Fire!"

Before he could draw another breath, Tom felt himself pressed into his seat as the *Polaris* quickly accelerated and curved up and away from the onrushing meteor in a long, smooth arc.

Captain Strong suddenly stepped through the hatch into the control deck. Glancing quickly at the scanner screen, he saw the white blip that was the meteor flashing away from the *Polaris* and he smiled.

"That was nice work, Corbett!" said Strong. "Get us back on course as soon as you can. Governor Hardy wants to get to Venusport as quickly as possible."

"Shall I tell Astro to pour on extra thrust, sir?" asked Tom.

"No, just maintain standard full space speed. No need to use emergency power unless it's really an emergency."

"Yes, sir," said Tom.

Strong walked around on the control deck, making a casual check of the ship's operation. But he knew he wouldn't find anything to complain about. Past experience had taught him that the three cadets kept a tight ship. At the sound of the hatch opening, he turned to see Governor Hardy standing just inside the hatch.

"I have to compliment you, Captain," Hardy said as he watched Tom operate the great control panel. "Your cadets really know their business. You've trained them well."

"Thank you, sir," replied Strong, "but they did it themselves. One thing I've learned since I've become an instructor at the Academy and that is you can't make a spaceman. He's born with the feeling and the instinct, or he isn't a spaceman."

Hardy nodded. "I've got some important messages to send out, Captain. I'd like to use the teleceiver for a while."

"Of course, sir," said Strong. "Right up that ladder there." The Solar Guard captain pointed to the ladder leading to the radar deck. "Manning's on duty now and will take care of you, sir."

"Thank you," said the governor, turning to the ladder.

A moment later, as Captain Strong and Tom were idly discussing the forthcoming screening operations on Venusport, they were surprised to see Roger climb down the ladder from the radar bridge.

"What are you doing down here, Manning?" inquired Strong. "I thought you were sending out messages for Governor Hardy."

Roger dropped into the co-control pilots' seat and shrugged. "The governor said he'd handle it. Said the messages were top secret and that he wouldn't *burden* me with their contents, since he knew how to operate a teleceiver!"

Puzzled, Tom looked at Roger. "What could be so secret about this mission?" he asked.

"I don't know," answered Roger. "After that speech the president of the Solar Council made the other night, the whole

Alliance must know about the project, the screening, and practically everything else."

Strong laughed. "You space brats see adventure and mystery in everything. Now, why wouldn't a man in charge of a project as large as this have secret messages? He might be talking to the president of the council!"

Tom blushed. "You're right, sir," he said. "I guess I let my imagination run riot."

"Just concentrate on getting this wagon to Venus in one piece, Corbett, and leave the secret messages to the governor," joked Strong. "And any time you get too suspicious, just remember that the governor was appointed head of this project by the Solar Alliance itself!"

Blasting through space, leaving a trail of atomic exhaust behind her, the *Polaris* rocketed smoothly through the dark void toward the misty planet of Venus. In rotating watches, the cadets ran the ship, ate, slept, and spent their few remaining spare hours attending to their classroom work with the aid of soundscribers and story spools. Each of them was working for the day when he would wear the black-and-gold uniform of the Solar Guard officer that was respected throughout the system as the mark of merit, hard work, distinction, and honor.

Once, Captain Strong and Astro donned space suits and went outside to inspect the hull of the *Polaris*. The ship had passed through a swarm of small meteorites, each less than a tenth of an inch in diameter but traveling at high speeds, and some had pierced the hull. It was a simple and quick job to seal the holes with a special atomic torch.

Like a giant silver bullet speeding toward a bull's-eye, the rocket ship pin-pointed the planet Venus from among the millions of worlds in space and was soon hovering over Venusport, nose up toward space, ready for a touchdown at the municipal spaceport. As the braking rockets quickly stopped all forward acceleration, the main rockets were cut in and the giant ship dropped toward the surface of the tropical planet tailfirst.

Tom's face glowed with excitement as he adjusted one lever and then another, delicately balancing the ship in its fall, meanwhile talking into the intercom and directing Astro in the careful reduction of thrust. On the radar deck Roger kept his eyes glued to the radar scanner and posted Tom on the altitude as the ship drew closer and closer to the ground.

"One thousand feet!" yelled Roger over the intercom. "Nine hundred—eight—seven—six—"

"Open main rockets one half!" called Tom. "Reduce rate of fall!"

The thunder of the rockets increased and the mighty ship quivered as its plummeting descent was checked slightly. Tom quickly adjusted the stabilizer trim tabs to keep the ship perpendicular to the ground, then watched the stern scanner carefully as the huge blast-pitted concrete ramp loomed larger and larger.

"Five hundred feet to touchdown," tolled Roger in more slow and measured tones. "Four hundred—three—two—"

On the scanner screen Tom could see the exhaust flare begin to lick at the concrete ramp, then splash its surface until it was completely hidden. He grasped the main control switch tightly and waited.

"One hundred feet," Roger's voice was tense now. "Seventy-five, fifty—"

Tom barked out a quick order. "Blast all rockets!"

In immediate response, the main tubes roared into thunderous life and the *Polaris* shook as the sudden acceleration battled the force of gravity. The ship's descent slowed perceptibly until she hovered motionless in the air, her stabilizer fins only two feet from the concrete ramp.

"Cut all power!" Tom's voice blasted through the intercom. A split second later there was a deafening silence, followed by a heavy muffled thud and the creak of straining metal as the *Polaris* came to rest on the ramp.

"Touchdown!" yelled Tom. He quickly cut all power to the control board and watched as one by one the gauges and dials registered zero or empty. The cadet stood up, noticed the time on the astral chronometer, and turned to face Captain Strong, rising from the chair beside him.

"Polaris made touchdown, planet Venus, at exactly 1543, sir," he said and saluted crisply.

Strong returned the salute. "Good work, Corbett," he said. "You handled her as though she was nothing more than a baby carriage!"

Roger came bouncing down the ladder, grinning. "Well," he said, "we're back on the planet where the monkeys walk around and call themselves men!"

"I heard that, Manning!" roared Astro, struggling through the hatch from the power deck. "One more crack like that and I'll stand you on your head and blast you off with your own space gas!"

"Listen, you overgrown Venusian ape," replied Roger, "I'll—"

"Yeah—" growled Astro, advancing on the smaller cadet. "You'll what?"

"All right, you two!" barked Strong. "Plug your jets! By the craters of Luna, one minute you act like hot-shot spacemen, and the next, you behave like children in a kindergarten!"

Suddenly the compartment echoed to hearty laughter. The cadets and their skipper turned to see Governor Hardy standing on the radar-bridge ladder, brief case in hand, roaring with laughter. He climbed down and faced the three cadets.

"If kindergarten behavior will produce spacemen like you, I'm all for it. Congratulations, all three of you. You did a good job!"

"Thank you, sir," said Tom.

Hardy turned to Strong. "Captain, I'm going ahead to the Solar Council building and get things set up for the screening. I imagine there are many anxious colonists ready to be processed!"

As Strong and the cadets came to attention and saluted, Governor Hardy turned and left the control deck.

Strong turned to the cadets. "From now on, you might as well forget that you're spacemen. Report to the Administration Building in one hour. You're going to do all your space jockeying in a chair from now on!"

* * * * *

For the next week, the three Space Cadets spent every waking hour in the Solar Council Administration Center, interviewing applicants who had passed their psychograph personality tests. Endlessly, from early morning until late at night, they questioned the eager applicants. Ninety-nine out of one hundred were refused. And when they were, they all had different reactions. Some cried, some were angry, some threatened, but the three cadets were unyielding. It was a thankless job, and after more than a week of it, tempers were on edge.

"What would you do," Roger would ask an applicant, "if you were suddenly drifting in space, in danger, and found that you had lost the vacuum in your audio tubes? How would you get help?"

Not one in over three hundred had realized that space itself was a perfect vacuum and could be substituted for the tubes. Roger had turned thumbs down on all of them.

Astro and Tom found their interviews equally as rough. One applicant admitted to Tom that he wanted to go to the satellite to establish a factory for making rocket juice, a highly potent drink that was not outlawed in the solar system, but was looked on with strong disfavor. When Tom turned down his application, the man tried to get Tom to enter into partnership with him, and when Tom refused, the man became violent and the cadet had to call enlisted Solar Guardsmen to throw him out.

While Tom and Roger made decisions quickly and decisively, Astro, on the other hand, patiently listened to all the tearful stories and sympathized with the applicants when they were unable to tear down a small reactor unit and rebuild it blindfolded. Painfully, sometimes with tears in his own eyes, he would tell the applicant he had failed, just when the would-be colonist would think Astro was going to pass him.

The three cadets were doing their jobs so well that in the one hundred and fifty-three applications approved by them Strong did not reject one, but sent them all on to Governor Hardy for final approval.

On the morning of the tenth day of screening, Hyram Logan and his family entered Roger's small office. A man of medium height with a thick shock of iron-gray hair and ruddy, weather-beaten features Logan looked as though he was used to working in the outdoors. Flanked by his son and daughter, he stood quietly before the desk as the young cadet, without looking up, scanned his application quickly.

"How old are the children?" asked Roger brusquely.

"I'm nineteen," replied a low musical voice, "and Billy's twelve."

Roger's head suddenly jerked up. He stared past Hyram Logan and a small towheaded boy, to gaze into the warm brown eyes of Jane Logan, a slender, pretty girl whose open, friendly features were framed by neatly combed reddish blond hair. Roger sat staring at her, openmouthed, until he heard a loud cough and saw Logan trying to hide a smile. He quickly turned back to the application.

"I see here you're a farmer, Mr. Logan," said Roger. He stole a glance at the young girl, but Billy saw him and winked. Roger flushed and turned to Logan as the older man answered his questioner.

"That's right," said Logan. "I'm a farmer. Been a farmer all my life."

"Why do you want to go to Roald, Mr. Logan?" asked Roger.

"Well," said Logan, "I have a nice piece of land south of Venusport a ways. Me and my wife developed it and we've been farming it for over twenty-five years. But my wife died last year and I just sort of lost heart in this place. I figured maybe that new satellite will give me a start again. You'll have to have farmers to feed the people. And I can farm anything from chemicals to naturals, in hard rock or muddy water." He paused and clamped his jaws together and said proudly, "My father was a farmer, and his father before him. One of the first to put a plow into Venusian topsoil!"

"Yes—uh—of course, Mr. Logan," mumbled Roger. "I don't think there'll—er—be any trouble about it."

The young cadet hadn't heard a word Hyram Logan had said, but instead had been gazing happily into the eyes of Jane Logan. He stamped the application and indicated the door to Tom's screening room, following the girl wistfully with his eyes. He muttered to himself, "There ought to be more applicants like Farmer Logan and his daughter for the brave new world of Roald!"

"And if there were, Cadet Manning," roared Captain Strong, standing in the doorway from the hall, "we'd probably wind up with a satellite filled with beautiful women!"

"Yes, sir! Er—no, sir," stuttered Roger, jerking himself to attention. "I mean, what's wrong with that?"

"By the rings of Saturn," declared Strong, "you'll never change, Manning!"

Roger grinned. "I hope not, sir."

The door to Tom's room opened and the curly-haired cadet walked in holding an application.

"Captain Strong," he said, "could I see you a minute?"

"Sure, Tom. Any trouble?" asked Strong.

Tom handed him the application silently and waited. Strong read the sheet and turned to Tom. "You know what to do in a case like this, Tom. Why come to me?"

Tom screwed up his face, thinking. "I don't know, sir. There's something different about this fellow. Astro passed him with flying colors. Said he knew as much about a reactor unit as he did. Roger passed him too."

"Who is it?" asked Roger. Strong handed him the paper.

"Sure, I passed him," said Roger. "That guy really knows his electronics."

Strong looked at Tom. "How do you feel about it, Tom?"

"Well, sir," began Tom, "I would pass him in a minute. He's had experience handling men and he's been in deep space before. He's logged an awful lot of time on merchant spaceships, but—"

"But what?" asked Strong. He took the paper and studied it again. "Looks to me as if he's what we're looking for," he said.

"I know, sir," said Tom. "But why would a man like that, with all that experience, want to bury himself on Roald? He could get practically any job he wants, right here in the system."

"Ummh," mused Strong. He reread the application. In the blank space for reason for going, the applicant had written simply:

Adventure. He handed the application back to Tom. "I think I see what you mean, Tom. It does look too good. Better not take a chance. Seven years is a long time to get stuck with a misfit, or worse, a—" He didn't finish, but Tom knew he meant a man not to be trusted.

"Tell Paul Vidac his application has been rejected," said Strong.

CHAPTER 4

"You mean Captain Strong has been recalled to the Academy?" gasped Roger.

"That's right," replied Tom. "He had a talk with Governor Hardy last night and this morning he took the jet liner back to Earth. Special orders from Commander Walters."

"Well, blast my jets!" exclaimed Astro. "Wonder what's up?"

"I don't know," said Tom. "But it must be something more important than the Roald project for him to pull out now!"

"It might have something to do with the project, Tom," suggested Roger.

Tom shook his head. "Maybe, but it just isn't like Captain Strong not to say anything to us before he left. I wouldn't have known about it if one of the enlisted guardsmen hadn't asked me if we were going with him."

Astro and Roger looked at each other. "You mean," asked Roger, "Captain Strong didn't tell you he was going?"

"That's just it!" replied Tom. "We've been traveling all over space together screening the applicants, and then Captain Strong just leaves when we start the final screening."

The three cadets were seated in a snack shop in Luna City on the Moon, sipping hot tea and eating spaceburgers. For six weeks they had been interviewing the applicants for the new satellite colony and were getting near the end. Their task had gone fairly smoothly except for some difficulty on Mars when Strong and the cadets had rejected scores of applicants with shady backgrounds; criminals and gamblers; spacemen who had had their space papers picked up for violation of the space code, and men who had been dismissed from the enlisted Solar Guard for serious misconduct. But now, finally, the quotas of all the colonies and planets but Luna

City on the Moon had been filled. Soon the expedition would blast off for Roald.

"Well," said Tom, sipping the last of his tea, "we have a heavy day ahead of us tomorrow. I guess we'd better get back to the *Polaris* and sack in."

"Yeah," agreed Astro, tossing some credits on the counter and following Tom and Roger out into the street. They walked past the shops, their blue cadet uniforms reflecting the garish colors of the nuanium signs in the shop windows. At the first corner they hailed a jet cab and were soon speeding out of the city toward the municipal spaceport.

The boys didn't talk much on the way out, each wondering why Captain Strong was recalled on such short notice, and why he had left without saying good-by to them. They knew they would see him in a few days when the processing of the Luna City applicants was over and they would return to Space Academy, but the relationship between the cadets and the Solar Guard captain had developed into a deeper association than just a cadet crew and officer supervisor. They were friends—spacemates! And the boys sensed trouble ahead when they arrived at the Luna City spaceport. They stood in the shadow of the *Polaris* and stared into the sky to watch the globe that was Earth revolve in the depths of space. The outline of the Western Hemisphere, flanked by the shimmering Atlantic and Pacific oceans, could be seen clearly. It was a breathtaking view of a world that had given birth to all the men who now took the travel from one world to another for granted.

"Gosh," said Tom, staring at the magnificent sight. "I see the Earth like that every time we blast off from Luna. I should be used to it by now, but—" he stopped suddenly and sighed.

"I know what you mean, Tom," said Astro. "It's the same with me. Gets me right here," and he put his hand to his heart.

"You don't know your anatomy yet, pal," drawled Roger. "Move your hand down a couple of inches. Things only get you in the stomach."

"Oh, is that a fact?" growled the big Venusian. Suddenly, without any apparent effort, he picked up the blond cadet and held him high in the air. "Which way shall I drop him, Tom? On his head or the seat of his pants? Seems to me it won't make much difference."

Tom laughed at the spectacle of Roger flailing the air helplessly, then suddenly stopped and grabbed Astro by the arm. "Wait, Astro," he called. "Look! There's someone in the ship!"

"What?" cried Astro, dropping Roger and turning to the *Polaris*. The three cadets saw light gleaming from the control-deck viewport.

"Well, I'll be a space monkey!" exclaimed Roger. "Who could it be?"

"I don't know," replied Tom. "Governor Hardy is at the Luna City Hotel, and Captain Strong is the only one besides us who has the light key to open the air lock!"

"Well, what're we waiting for!" said Roger. "Let's find out what's going on!"

The three cadets climbed into the ship and raced up the companionway to the control deck.

"No one here," announced Roger as he stepped through the hatch. He turned to Astro. "You were the last one out of the ship. Are you sure you locked it up?"

"The ship was locked, Cadet Manning!" said a voice in back of them. The three cadets whirled around to face a tall, wiry man with dark hair, dressed in civilian clothes and holding a cup of coffee. He smiled at the three startled cadets and casually drained the cup. "I opened her," he continued in a deep voice. "Governor Hardy gave me the key."

"Who are you?" asked Tom, almost indignant at the man's self-assurance. And then he stopped, frowning, "Say, haven't I seen you before?"

"You're right, Tom," cried Astro. "I've seen him too!"

"Who are you, mister?" demanded Roger.

The man turned back to the messroom just off the control deck, put the coffee cup down on the table, and returned to face the three cadets. "My name is Paul Vidac. I'm the new lieutenant governor of Roald."

"You're what?" gasped Tom.

"You're space happy!" exclaimed Roger. "Your application was refused. Captain Strong rejected it himself."

"Fortunately for the project of Roald," said Vidac with a half-smile playing at his lips, "Captain Strong has been taken off the

Roald project." He paused and lounged against the bulkhead to announce, "I have replaced him."

"You couldn't replace Captain Strong digging a hole in the ground, mister!" snapped Roger sarcastically.

"You might have taken over his work, but you couldn't touch him with an atomic blaster," growled Astro. "Captain Strong is—"

"Wait, fellows," said Tom. "Let's find out what this is all about."

"That's all right, Corbett," Vidac broke in. "I appreciate your allegiance. I wouldn't like anyone who would accept another person in place of a friend without putting up a beef." His voice was as smooth as the purr of a cat.

"How could you have replaced him, mister?" asked Tom, with just a little more self-control than Roger or Astro had shown.

"Very simple," said Vidac. "Governor Hardy has the final say on all applications, as you know. He has unquestioned authority to appoint, approve, and select anyone he wants. In view of my experience, Governor Hardy was delighted to have me join the Roald expedition."

The three cadets looked at each other in bewilderment. Finally Tom walked over and stuck out his hand. "We're glad to have you aboard, sir." He managed a smile.

Reluctantly Roger and Astro followed suit.

"Thank you, boys," said Vidac with a smile. "I'm sure we'll learn to work together smoothly in these last few days. There are a few changes to be made of course. But it really doesn't matter. You'll be finished with the screening soon."

"What kind of changes, sir?" asked Tom.

"Oh, just routine," answered Vidac. "Instead of you seeing the applicants first, I will speak with each one briefly before sending them on to you."

"What's the matter with the way we've been doing it?" asked Roger with a slight edge to his voice that did not go unnoticed. Vidac looked at the cadet. His mouth was smiling, but his eyes were hard.

"I think, Cadet Manning," purred Vidac, "that it will be better for you not to question me, or any of my practices. A Space Cadet's first rule is to take orders, *not* to question them."

Tom was thinking quickly. It was obvious that Vidac had gone straight to Governor Hardy and had prevailed on him to review his application. Tom could see how Vidac's background would impress the governor. He remembered that there wasn't any real evidence against Vidac. In fact, Tom thought, it was only because Vidac's background was so superior to most of the applicants that he had aroused suspicion at all. Now, with Captain Strong recalled to the Academy, it was only natural for the governor to get the best man for the job. Tom was ready to admit that Vidac's background certainly spoke for itself.

He looked at the man and grinned. "I'll tell you honestly, sir. When Captain Strong refused your application, it was because—well—"

Vidac was watching Tom shrewdly. "Well?" he asked quietly.

"It was because we couldn't understand how a man like you would want to bury yourself on a satellite for seven years when you could get most any kind of job you would want, right here in the Alliance."

Vidac hesitated just a second, and then his face broke into a broad grin. "You know, Corbett, you're right! Absolutely right! I can see where you three boys have done a fine job for the governor." He slapped Astro on the back and threw his arm around Tom's shoulder, speaking to them in a suddenly confidential tone. "As a matter of fact, I was offered the directorship of the Galactic space lanes only last week," he said. "Do you know why I refused it?"

Tom shook his head.

"Because I'm a spaceman, just like yourselves." He looked at Astro. "Cadet Astro, would you take a job with an outfit and give up space to sit behind a desk eight hours a day?"

"No, sir!" said Astro emphatically.

"Well, that's exactly the way I feel. But I commend you on your observations about me, Corbett. I think I would have been a little suspicious myself."

The three cadets smiled.

"Thank you, sir," said Tom. "And forget what we just said. If Governor Hardy's okayed you, that's good enough for us."

"Thanks, Corbett," said Vidac. "I appreciate that."

"I guess we'd better turn in now," said Roger. "We have a hard day ahead of us. Those applicants come at you like dinosaurs."

"Right!" said Vidac. "I'll take over Captain Strong's quarters. See you in the morning."

The three cadets went to their quarters without saying a word. When the hatch was closed, Roger turned and faced his unit mates.

"Well, it sure looks like we made a mistake about that spaceman!" he said. "I think he's all right!"

"Yeah," said Astro, "you can't blame a guy for not wanting to take a desk job."

Tom merely sat in his bunk, starting to pull off one of his soft leather space boots. He held it a moment, thinking, and then looked up at his two unit mates. "You know, I think I'm going to have a talk with the governor."

"About what?" asked Roger.

"Vidac," said Tom simply.

"What could you say that he doesn't already know?" asked Astro.

"Why—" Tom stopped. After a moment he dropped his boot to the deck, looked up at Roger and Astro, and smiled. "Nothing, I guess."

"Come on," said Roger, yawning. "Let's turn in. Just the thought of facing those applicants tomorrow makes me tired."

Astro turned out the light and hopped into bed. Tom lay in his bunk, hands under his head, wondering about Vidac, and then he began to think about the colony of Roald. He lay a long time, thinking about the fine people who were giving up comfortable homes, successful businesses. He thought of Hyram Logan and family; the shopkeeper from Titan with three sets of twin boys; the Martian miner who had spent twenty-five futile years searching for uranium in the asteroid belt. They were all ready to go over fifty billion miles into deep space and begin their lives again. Tom shook his head. He wondered if he had a choice whether he would chance the mystery and danger of deep space.

With the steady hum of the electronic generator on the power deck droning in his ears the curly-haired cadet soon fell asleep.

* * * * *

"What did you say your name was?" asked Roger of the applicant standing before him. He was a man badly in need of a shave and his clothes looked as if he had slept in them. He was the sixty-sixth applicant Roger had seen that morning.

"Tad Winters," replied the man in a surly tone, "and hurry up with this business. I haven't got all day!"

Roger looked up sharply. "You'll wait until I've had time to check your application, sir. Or you can leave right now!"

"Listen, punk," snarled Winters, "I just saw your boss—"

"My boss?" asked Roger, puzzled.

"Yeah," said Winters. "Your boss, Vidac! And he said I was to tell you to pass me!"

Roger stood up and looked the man in the eye. "You've had your space papers suspended twice, Mr. Winters. Once for smuggling, and once for insubordination on a deep-space merchantman. Your application to go to Roald is rejected."

"We'll see about that!" growled Winters. "Gimme that, you space jerk!" He snatched the application out of Roger's hand and stomped out of the room.

Roger smiled. It was nothing new to him for the applicants to threaten him and seek higher authority. He buzzed for the next applicant.

Meanwhile, Tom was interviewing a small man with heavy eyebrows and a thin face. One side of his mouth twitched continually, making the man look as though he were laughing. Tom read over the application and looked up quickly.

"Mr. Bush," said Tom, "you've stated here that you were once a messenger for the Spaceways Bonded Messenger Service and that you were dismissed. Why was that?"

Ed Bush's mouth twitched as he played with his hat and stirred uneasily in his chair. "I was framed," he said finally.

"Framed?" asked Tom.

"Yeah, framed!" snapped Bush. "I was taking a credit pouch to Venusport from Atom City when it was stolen from me."

"Could you prove it?" asked Tom.

"How could I prove it when I don't know what happened to it?" growled Bush. "Listen, Corbett, you can't hold a little thing like that against me. A man is entitled to one mistake—"

Tom held up his hand. "Mr. Bush, you also had your space papers suspended for six months and were caught during the suspension blasting off with false papers. Was that a mistake?"

"Well, what do you expect a man to do? Go hungry? I've been a spaceman longer than you've been alive. I had to have a job. There wasn't anything else I could do." His voice trailed off into a whine.

"But you did, willfully and with full knowledge of your act, violate the space code by using false papers, didn't you?" pursued Tom.

"Yeah, but—" whined Bush.

"I'm sorry," said Tom, standing up. "Your application has been rejected."

Bush stood up and snatched the application from Tom. His mouth began to twitch furiously. "Why, you little—"

"That's enough, Bush!" snapped Vidac, who had suddenly entered the room. "Leave your application on the desk and get out!"

Bush turned and looked at Vidac, nodded, and glared at Tom before stalking from the room. Vidac smiled at Tom's questioning look and walked over. He sat on the edge of Tom's desk and picked up Bush's application.

"Funny thing about Bush, Tom," Vidac mused.

"What, sir?" asked Tom.

"Notice the nervous twitch he has on the side of his face?"

"Yes, sir," said Tom.

"I've known Bush a long time. Many years. He used to be the happiest little space joker in the system, singing all the time, playing a concertina. And then he lost that credit pouch. It bothered him real bad."

"I guess it would, sir," said Tom.

"And then he got caught blasting off with false papers and of course that made him a marked man. He developed the nervous twitch right after that. He's a good man, Tom. And I think we ought to give him another chance."

Tom gasped. "But, sir, he's broken the space code!"

Vidac looked at Tom and smiled. "I know, Tom, and it's a serious thing. But I think he deserves another chance."

"We've refused people for a lot less than that, sir," said Tom emphatically, "before you came."

Vidac's face hardened. "I said we were going to give him another chance!"

Tom met the lieutenant governor's eyes coolly. "Yes, sir." He stamped the application and handed it to Vidac.

"It's pretty easy to sit in judgment of others, Tom," said Vidac, smiling again. "If there are any more—ah—questionable applicants, I suggest you send them to me. And if I want to give them another chance, you will, of course, follow orders."

"Very well, sir," replied Tom, tight-lipped. "If you say so."

Vidac's eyes hardened. *"I say so,* Corbett!" He turned and walked from the room.

Tom sat down weakly. As he was about to buzz for the next applicant, the door burst open and Roger came into the room. The blond-haired cadet's lips were pulled tight in a grim line.

"There's something rocket-blasting screwy around here, Tom!" he exclaimed.

"What do you mean?" asked Tom.

"I just rejected a real low-down space crawler—a guy named Tad Winters."

"Yes?" Tom was alert, anticipating Roger's answer.

"He went to Vidac and came back later with his application approved."

Tom slammed his fist on the desk. "That proves it! Governor Hardy has to be told what's going on!" He flipped on the teleceiver near by and asked the central communications operator to connect him with the governor's office. In a moment the face of Christopher Hardy sharpened into focus on the screen.

"What is it, Corbett?" asked the governor.

"I'd like to talk to you, sir, if I may. Something's just come up and I'm not sure what to do."

"Well, whatever it is, I'm sure Governor Vidac will be able to take care of it. Speak to him."

Tom gulped and glanced at Roger. "But, sir," he stammered, "it's—it's—"

"It's what, Corbett? Hurry, lad! I haven't got all day."

"What I have to say is—is—about the lieutenant governor, sir," Tom managed finally.

"Now listen, son," said Hardy, "I have a lot of confidence in you three boys. You've all done a fine job. But I screened Mr. Vidac myself, and I'm satisfied that he is just the man I need. After Captain Strong was recalled to the Academy, I had to have a man to take over for him. And I am satisfied that Mr. Vidac is about as fine a man as I could get! Now don't bother me again. You've done a fine job, as I said. But don't let it go to your heads!"

"Yes, sir," said Tom, clamping his teeth together. "Very well, sir!"

"One more thing," said Hardy. "We've about finished here at Luna City. When you've processed the last of the applicants, prepare the *Polaris* for a return trip to Space Academy." He paused and smiled. "I think I might be able to convince Commander Walters you need a two weeks' leave!" He smiled again and then his face disappeared from the screen.

Tom looked up at Roger. "I don't like it, Roger. Maybe I'm wrong, but either the governor is pretty dumb or Vidac is the slickest thing in space!"

"Could be both," drawled Roger.

Tom looked at the pile of applications on his desk, and then at the door to Vidac's office.

"Whatever it is, we've got to tell Captain Strong!"

CHAPTER 5

"For the last time, Captain Strong has been sent on a special mission to Pluto!" said the supervisory officer at the Academy. "Now stop bothering me or I'll log all three of you with twenty galley demerits!"

"Very well, sir," said Tom. "But could you tell us if the mission had anything to do with the Roald project?"

"Cadet Corbett," replied the officer wearily, "even if I knew I couldn't tell you. It was a special order from Commander Walters' office. Captain Strong blasted off three days ago with a full crew of guardsmen in a rocket cruiser."

"And he didn't—" began Roger.

"And he didn't leave any message for you," concluded the officer.

"Thank you, sir," said Tom. "Come on, fellows, let's go. We've got to blast off for Mars in half an hour and we haven't got our gear packed."

The officer watched the three cadets leave and then called after them. "If Captain Strong returns before you get back from Mars, Corbett, I'll ask him to leave a message!"

"Thanks, sir," said Tom.

The three boys left the Tower building and hopped on a slidewalk for the spaceport. The Academy was buzzing with activity as Solar Guard officers, scientists, and enlisted men attended to the millions of details of the mass flight of the colonists into deep space.

They met Mike McKenny, the stubby warrant officer, at the air lock of the Solar Guard rocket destroyer that would take them to Mars. After they had climbed into the ship, they waited for a full hour before they could get clearance to blast off. And, in flight, they were forced to maintain constant alert and careful position in the heavy flow of traffic to and from Earth.

"Never saw the Academy so busy in all my life," commented Mike. "Must be a thousand ships there and in the Atom City fitting docks."

"Yeah," agreed Roger. "This is going to be some push!"

The Solar Guard worked late into the night, examining every ship in the Alliance

From Mars, Titan, Ganymede, Luna City, Venus, the Asteroid Colonies, and as far away as the uranium mines of Pluto, the colonists arrived, to be quartered at Space Academy. Excited, and anxious to begin their new life, they assembled for their antibiotic shots and the last medical check by the Solar Guard doctors. There were crystal miners from Titan, farmers from Venus, Mars, and Earth, prospectors from the New Sahara desert of Mars, engineers from the atmosphere booster stations on Ganymede, and just plain citizens who wanted a new life on the distant satellite of Wolf 359. All had gathered for the great mass flight into space.

At the same time the giant fleet of ships needed to carry the colonists to Roald was being assembled. Officers of the Solar Guard worked late into the night, examining the construction of every ship in the Alliance for use in the flight to Roald. If a jet liner or merchantman was found to be satisfactory, it was purchased at full price from the owners and flown to refitting docks at Space Academy and Atom City where work was begun converting it to a special use. Every ship was to be cannibalized on Roald, its hull taken apart to provide housing and its power decks converted into electropower plants. Now working with Mike McKenny, the three Space Cadets were part of a large group of transfer crews engaged in flying ships to Earth.

Returning from Mars, where they had picked up a giant jet liner, the three cadets landed on the crowded Academy spaceport and turned hopefully to Mike.

"You think we can get a twenty-four-hour pass, Mike?" asked Roger.

"Yeah," growled Astro. "Governor Hardy promised us a two-week leave, but I guess he got swamped under details!"

Mike scratched his head. "I don't know, boys," he said. "I can't give it to you, but I'll speak to Commander Walters for you. I know it's been a pretty rough grind for all of you."

"Thanks, Mike," said Tom. "We'd appreciate it."

Later, when the three boys had signed over the giant ship to the refitting crews, they headed for their dormitory for a refreshing shower.

As Astro began to strip off his jacket, he suddenly asked, "Do you think Captain Strong has returned from Pluto yet?"

"I doubt it," answered Roger. "I'm sure there would have been a message for us on the chatter wire if he had." Roger referred to a tape recorder that was standard equipment in each of the dormitory rooms, used expressly for messages.

"You know something," said Tom. "I think we ought to go directly to Commander Walters about Vidac."

"Commander Walters!" growled Astro. "Are you off your rocket?"

"Why shouldn't we?" agreed Roger.

"I'll tell you why!" said Astro. "Commander Walters probably is so busy you couldn't get near him with a six-inch atomic blaster. And what are we going to say after we get there? Just that Vidac has let some space crawlers into the expedition?"

"That's enough, isn't it?" asked Roger.

"We can't let this slide, Astro," said Tom determinedly. "Somebody's got to do something about Vidac, and if the governor won't, it should be brought to Commander Walters' attention."

"Come on. Let's do it right now," urged Roger. "We'll be sticking our necks out, but since when have we ever let that stop us?"

Astro shrugged his shoulders and quickly redressed. The three boys left the dormitory building and started hopping from one slidewalk to another, as they made their way to the Tower building. All around them the activity of the Academy seemed to have increased. Everyone seemed to be rushing somewhere. Even the green-clad Earthworm cadets had been pressed into service as messengers. And mixed in with the officials were the colonists wandering around sight-seeing.

"Say!" exclaimed Astro. "Isn't that Jane Logan?"

"Where?" asked Roger. Astro pointed to a parallel slidewalk where the girl colonist from Venus was being whisked along in the same direction. "Well, blast my jets!" cried Roger. "So it is!"

"Relax, Roger," said Astro with a wink at Tom. "Business before pleasure!"

"Yeah—yeah, but this is business too," said Roger, jumping lightly to the near-by slidewalk beside the pretty young colonist.

"Well," he exclaimed, "if it isn't the little space doll from Venus!"

Jane Logan turned around and smiled. "Well, Cadet Manning!" And seeing Astro and Tom come up, she smiled a greeting to them. "And Cadets Astro and Corbett!"

"Never mind them," said Roger. "I'm the only one that counts."

"Why, Cadet Manning," said the girl archly, "I had no idea you were so important."

"As a matter of fact, I'm going up to see Commander Walters right now on some important business."

"Commander Walters?" gasped Jane. "Ohhhh!"

Roger grinned. "Sure, and while I'm up there, I'll get a twenty-four-hour pass and we'll take in the sights at Atom City tonight. O.K.?"

"Well, I don't know what my father would say about that!"

"Ah, tell him you're going to go out with me," said Roger, "and there won't be any trouble."

"Psst! Roger!" Astro hissed suddenly, punching Roger in the ribs. Roger gave the big cadet a frowning look and turned back to Jane.

"We'll have dinner, and then see a stereo, and I know a nice quiet spot where we can talk—"

"Talk?" demanded a gruff voice behind Roger.

The cadet whirled to find himself staring into the grim face of Hyram Logan. "Just what would you talk about, Cadet Manning?" demanded Jane's father. Billy stood at his father's side, grinning broadly.

"Uh—er—ah—radar, sir, the—er—problems we find in radar."

Logan turned to Jane. "Are you interested in radar, Jane?"

"Not particularly, Father," said Jane, a twinkle in her eye. Tom and Astro were trying unsuccessfully to stifle their laughter.

His face suddenly flushing crimson, Roger looked around and stammered, "I—uh—I just remembered—got to see a feller about a hot rocket!" And Roger jumped off the slidewalk to disappear into the Tower building.

Laughing out loud now, Tom and Astro said good-by to Jane and her father and followed Roger.

Inside the gleaming Tower of Galileo, the two boys raced up the slidestairs and caught up with Roger.

"Well, Romeo," said Astro, slapping him on the back, "that was what I call a strategic retreat in the face of overwhelming odds."

"Ah, go blast your jets!" snarled Roger.

"Never mind, Roger," said Tom, "we probably won't get the pass, anyway."

Suppressing smiles, Astro and Tom followed Roger down the long corridor toward the office of Commander Walters. In the anteroom they waited while an aide announced them to the commander. Standing before the aide's desk, they could see the commander's face come into focus on the small teleceiver screen, and they were alarmed to see Governor Hardy seated beside him.

"What is it, Sergeant?" asked Commander Walters.

"Cadets Corbett, Manning, and Astro of the *Polaris* unit to see you, sir," said the enlisted guardsman.

"Send them right in," said Walters.

The aide flipped off the teleceiver and smiled up at the cadets. "Go ahead, fellows. He's in a good mood today, so you don't have to worry about demerits."

Tom thanked the guardsman and started for the door to the inner office, but Roger grabbed him by the arm and pulled him back.

"We can't go in there now, Tom," he whispered. "Not with Governor Hardy sitting there!"

"I know," replied Tom. "But we can't back out now. He's been told we're here. We'll just go in and ask him for the week-end pass."

"Good idea," agreed Astro.

"Say, are you guys going in or not?" called the sergeant.

The three cadets nodded quickly and stepped inside the room. Governor Hardy and the commander were studying a blueprint which was spread out on the desk. The three cadets came to attention in front of the desk as Walters looked up inquiringly.

"Polaris unit reporting on a special privilege request, sir," announced Tom.

Walters smiled. "Yes, I know why you're here, boys. Warrant Officer McKenny spoke to me a little while ago. Here's your pass. After the job you've done, you deserve it." He held out the slip of paper.

Governor Hardy stood up and snapped his fingers. "You know, Commander, I owe these boys an apology. When we left Luna City, I promised them that I would speak to you about giving them a two-weeks' leave, and it completely slipped my mind!"

"It's a good thing it did," said Walters. "I've had these boys doing some important work and I'll have even more need for them now. Come here, boys. I want you to look at something." He waved them around his desk and pointed to the blueprint on his desk. Tom, Roger, and Astro gasped. It was the plan for a large city.

"That will be the first settlement on Roald," said Walters. "You boys will be remembered for a long time to come." He looked up at the governor and winked.

"How is that, sir?" asked Tom.

Walters placed his finger on the many intersecting lines in the blueprint that designated streets. "Each of these streets, avenues, roads, and expressways will be named after a member of the first colonial expedition to Roald. Your names will be among them."

"Ours!" exclaimed Tom. "Does that mean that—"

"I've been talking to Governor Hardy," Walters continued casually. "He tells me you've done a fine job. I think a tour of duty as cadet observers on Roald will just about round out your training."

The three boys looked at each other, eyes wide with surprise and pleasure.

"We'll actually go with the colonists?" asked Astro.

"That's right, Cadet Astro," said Walters. "And I'm sorry that I can't give you more than a twenty-four-hour pass. But time is very short."

"Twenty-four hours will be fine, sir," said Tom. "And we appreciate your giving us the opportunity to go to Roald."

"It won't be easy, Corbett," cautioned Walters. "You'll have to work harder than you've worked before. You'll have to maintain your studies and I'll expect you to send back a report every month." He turned to Governor Hardy. "Do you have anything to add, sir?"

"Not a thing, Commander," replied Hardy. "I've worked with these boys for weeks and I know what to expect of them. I know I can depend on them to take orders."

"All right," said Walters, turning to the cadets. "Go to Atom City and have yourself a good time. Report back to the Academy tomorrow at eighteen hundred hours. Unit dismissed!"

The three cadets saluted and left the room. In the corridor they slumped against the wall.

"That," announced Roger, "is as close as I ever want to come to getting a rocket shell in the side of the head."

"You can say that again, spaceboy," sighed Astro.

"Just think what would have happened if we'd opened our mouths about Vidac!"

"Come on," said Tom. "We've got twenty-four hours to soak up as much of this Earth as we can. And I, for one, am going to have a good time!"

Without a word, the three cadets left the Tower building and made their way to the monorail station, where they would catch the streamlined express to Atom City. Each of the cadets was acutely aware of the trouble that lay ahead of them, and with Captain Strong at the outer edge of the solar system on a long haul to Pluto, not even a miracle could get him back to Space Academy in time to help them.

CHAPTER 6

A thousand spaceships, freighters, converted luxury liners, auxiliary supply vessels, rocket cruisers, destroyers and scouts, all led by the *Polaris*, blasted in even formation through the last charted regions of the solar system. Inside the gleaming ships the colonists had settled down for the long voyage to the new satellite of Roald. Their quarters were cramped and uncomfortable. There was very little to do and their only entertainment was the shipboard stereos. Many spent endless hours at the long-range telescanners watching the sun star Wolf 359, seeing it come closer and closer.

Aboard the *Polaris*, Tom, Roger, and Astro worked an endless tour of duty, maneuvering the great fleet of ships into ordered formation so that any vessel could be found without difficulty. Now that the fleet was in position, and the early confusion of forming up was over, they had hoped for a little rest, but were disappointed when Vidac suddenly ordered them to report to his quarters.

Standing at the hatch outside of Vidac's room, Tom and Roger waited for Astro as he climbed up the ladder to join them. The big cadet finally made the top and stood breathing heavily.

"By the rings of Saturn," he grumbled, "I'm so tired I could sleep right here. Right now!"

"Yeah," growled Roger. "You'd think Vidac would give us a break after what we've done."

"We'll have plenty of time to rest on this trip," said Tom. "This is just the beginning. I'll bet by the time we reach Roald we'll be wishing we had something to do to pass away the time."

He turned and pressed the annunciator button and the hatch slid open. The three cadets entered the room and snapped to attention.

"Polaris unit reporting as ordered, sir," said Tom.

Vidac swung around in his chair and stared up at the three cadets, a hint of a smile curling his lips.

"You've done a fine job, boys," he said. "The fleet is in good formation." He paused as he settled back in his chair. "But I'm not the one who believes in idle hands. I've assigned you to Professor Sykes. He needs help in charting the unexplored regions of space we're approaching. And you three need that kind of training. Report to him in one hour."

"One hour," gasped Roger. "But we're completely blasted out!"

"Yes, sir," agreed Astro. "Couldn't we log some sack time before we start another assignment?"

Vidac stood up and faced them. "You might as well learn right now," he said sharply, "that when I give an order I expect it to be carried out without suggestions, complaints, or whining excuses!"

"But—!" stammered Roger.

Tom quickly stepped forward. His back ramrod straight, he saluted the lieutenant governor. "We understand, sir."

He executed a perfect about-face and, followed by Astro and Roger, he left the lieutenant governor's quarters.

Outside, the three cadets walked wearily toward the messroom just off the control deck. After preparing a hasty cup of tea, they sat about the table silently, each thinking about the long trip ahead of them and the difficulties they were sure to encounter with Vidac. They all three jumped when Jeff Marshall, Professor Sykes's aide, entered and boomed a cheerful greeting.

"Hi, fellas!"

"Hiya," muttered Tom. Astro and Roger merely nodded.

"Say!" cried Jeff, his usually cheerful face showing concern. "What's the matter with you three guys? You look as though someone told you there isn't any Moon!"

"Worse than that," said Roger. "Vidac just assigned us to work with Professor Sykes on charting the new space regions."

Jeff smiled. "Nothing wrong with that. The old professor isn't so bad. He sounds worse than he really is."

"Listen," growled Astro, "you don't have to tell me what Professor Sykes is like. I had a class with him at the Academy. That guy is so sour, vinegar is sweet by comparison."

Astro's outburst was said with such fierce conviction that Tom, Roger, and Jeff burst out laughing.

"It isn't that we mind working with Professor Sykes," said Tom. "He's a real brain and we could learn a lot from him, but—"

"But what?" asked Jeff.

"It's the way Vidac has suddenly—well, taken over around here. We're supposed to be under the direct orders of Governor Hardy."

"Well, Vidac is Hardy's executive officer," said Jeff.

"Yeah," muttered Roger. "We're finding that out, the hard way."

"I still can't understand why Governor Hardy would make him lieutenant governor, with his background," mused Tom.

Jeff grinned. "You three guys have been jockeying with so many space crawlers since you came to the Academy, you're suspicious of everyone you meet. I'm surprised you haven't decided that I'm an arch space criminal myself!"

The three cadets smiled. Jeff Marshall was so gentle and mild, his manner so quietly humorous, it was impossible to picture him as any kind of a criminal.

During the few minutes they had left, they casually discussed the chances of the senior space cadets against the enlisted guardsmen in a forthcoming mercuryball game, and then went up to the forward compartment of the *Polaris*, which served as a temporary observatory for Professor Sykes.

The Chief Astrophysicist of Space Academy, Professor Barnard Sykes, was a man of great talent and even greater temper. Referred to as Barney by the cadet corps, he was held in high regard and downright fear. There were few cadets who had escaped his scathing tongue when they had made a mistake and practically the entire student body had, at one time or another, singly and in unison, devoutly wished that a yawning hole would open up and swallow them when he began one of his infamous tirades. Even perfection in studies and execution by a cadet would receive a mere grunt from the cantankerous professor. Such temperament was permissible at the Academy by an instructor only because of his genius and for no other reason. And Professor Sykes fitted the bill. It was by sheer devotion to his work and single-mindedness of purpose that he was able to become a leading scientist in his field. Professor Sykes had been assigned, at his request, to the Roald expedition. As the leading scientist, it was his job to evaluate every new discovery made during the trip out to the distant satellite, and later make observations on the colony itself. Scientifically, and in a sense ultimately, the success or failure of the Roald expedition would rest on his round hunched shoulders.

When the three cadets and Jeff Marshall entered the observatory, they found Professor Sykes bending over a calculating machine checking some figures. Apparently finding a mistake, he muttered to himself angrily and started over again. Roger stepped forward.

"I can handle a calculator pretty well, sir," Roger said. "You want me to do it for you?"

Sykes whirled around and glared at the blond-haired cadet. "What's your name?" he snapped.

"Why—Cadet Manning, sir," replied Roger.

"Cadet Manning, do you see this calculator?" Sykes pointed to the delicate instrument that could add, subtract, divide, and multiply, in fractions and whole numbers, as well as measure the light years in sidereal time.

"Yes, sir," said Roger.

"Cadet Manning," continued Sykes, "I perfected that machine. Built the first one myself. Now offhand, wouldn't you say I would know how to operate it?"

"Yes, sir," stammered Roger. "But I just wanted to help, sir."

"When I need your help I'll ask for it!" snorted the little professor. He turned to Jeff. "What are they doing here? You know I don't like to be interrupted when I'm making observations!"

Jeff smiled slowly. "They've been assigned to work with you, sir. They're your new assistants."

"My assistants!" screamed Sykes. "What space-blasting idiot got the idea that I needed any assistants?"

"The lieutenant governor, sir," said Jeff.

"Oh, he did, did he!" Sykes turned to the teleceiver, flipped it on, and waited impatiently for the machine to warm up.

In a moment Vidac's face came into view. Before the lieutenant governor could say a word, Sykes began to scream at him.

"What's the idea of sending these brainless Space Cadets to me! Assistants—bah! Can't you find something else for them to do?" bawled Sykes. "Is my work considered so unimportant that I should be impeded by these—these—" He sputtered and turned to wave at Tom, Roger, and Astro who still stood at rigid attention.

Sykes got no further. Vidac simply cut off his televiser and left the professor staring into a blank screen. His face became beet red, and he screamed at Jeff Marshall. "Get them out of here! Put them to work—scrubbing the decks, cleaning up the place, anything! But keep them out of my way!" Then wagging a finger in Roger's face, he screamed his last warning. "Don't ever speak to me again, unless I speak to you *first!*"

Smarting under the continuous blast of anger from the professor, Roger could no longer restrain himself. Slowly, with the calm deliberate manner and slow casual drawl that characterized him at his sarcastic best, the cadet stepped forward. He saluted, and with his face a bare six inches from Sykes, said evenly, "To speak to you, sir, under any conditions, sir, would be such a stroke of bad luck, sir, that I wouldn't wish it on the last spaceman in the world, sir." With another curt salute he wheeled smartly and walked out of the room.

Flabbergasted, Professor Sykes could manage no more than a hoarse bubbling sound and he finally turned to Jeff Marshall, waving his arms violently. "Get them out of here—get them out of here. Get them out!"

The sergeant nodded quickly at Tom and Astro, who, repressing smiles, saluted and followed Roger out of the observatory.

Within the hour, Professor Sykes was still screaming loudly, this time to Governor Hardy himself. Standing before his desk the eccentric scientist babbled his complaint of Vidac's rebuff and Roger's outrageous insolence.

"I won't stand for it, Governor! My work is more important than having to wipe the noses of three loudmouthed sassy cadets! And as for that—that man Vidac, if he ever turns off the teleceiver again when I'm talking to him, I'll go to the Solar Council itself. I'm an officer of the Solar Guard and demand respect!"

His harangue concluded, Sykes turned and stalked toward the hatch.

"Just a moment," called Hardy, stepping around the desk to confront the little scientist. "All of us are assigned to important jobs," he said calmly. "Yours is scientific research; the cadets have a specific job of education; I am the co-ordinator of the whole project and Lieutenant Governor Vidac is my immediate executive officer. We all have to work together. Let's see if we can't do it a little more smoothly, eh?" Hardy smiled and turned back to his chair. "But one thing more, Sykes. If there are any more petty disagreements, please settle them with Vidac. Don't come up here again, unless I order you to!"

"You order *me,"* gasped Sykes.

"That's all, Sykes!" said Hardy coldly, picking up some papers in an obvious gesture of dismissal. His fury redoubled, the professor backed out of the room and hurried below to Vidac's quarters. Expecting another cold interview, he was surprised when Vidac met him with a smile and asked him to enjoy a cup of coffee with him.

"No need for us to antagonize each other over the foolish mistakes and bunglings of the cadets, Professor," said Vidac evenly. "I apologize for cutting you off, but I make it a point never to talk to a man when he's angry. Come, sit down, and have a cup of coffee. I'm sure we can work out the answer." He paused and then added pointedly, "Without bothering Governor Hardy."

"Yes—yes—of course," said Sykes, accepting the proffered cup.

Within a half-hour, Vidac had Sykes laughing at his jokes and stories, and when they parted, the professor's temper had abated. When the scientist finally left, Vidac turned to the ship's intercom and paged the cadets. A few minutes later they entered his quarters for the second time that evening.

Vidac was ready and waiting when they entered the room and came to attention. He leaned back against his desk and looked at each cadet through half-closed eyes. Finally, after a full minute of silence, he began to speak.

"I gave you specific instructions to report to Professor Sykes for work as his assistants," he said in a cold, hard voice. "I also told you I wanted my order carried out without complaints or whining excuses. You saw fit to start an argument as soon as you reported, thereby interrupting his work. The professor went to the governor and interrupted *his* work. The professor came to see me, interrupting *my* work. Three men had to stop their jobs because you didn't feel like carrying out orders."

"But, sir—" said Tom. "The professor—"

"Shut up, Corbett!" said Vidac coldly. "Don't ever interrupt me again while I'm talking!"

"Yes, sir!" said Tom through tight lips.

"You boys have been enjoying considerable latitude under Captain Strong. But I would like to remind you that Captain Strong isn't here. There's no one here but me. You will do as I say, when I say it, and as long as I say it. If you don't, I promise you, you will regret it."

"May I speak, sir?" asked Roger.

"No, Manning. I've heard about your tongue. I warn you, never use it on me, or—" He paused. "Just never use it, that's all."

He walked about the room, but kept his eyes on the cadets. "There's just one more thing I want you to understand, before you're dismissed. I know that all three of you refused my application as a colonist originally. I know what your feelings must be now that I am your superior. And because I know, I feel I should warn you not to try to express your feelings. You can't win. You can only lose. If

I ever catch you going to Governor Hardy, by-passing my authority, I'll make your lives so miserable you'll wish you were dead. Now get out of here!"

As one man, the cadets of the *Polaris* unit saluted, turned a perfect about-face, and walked once again from the room. Outside in the passageway, they relaxed and headed for their quarters.

None of them could say a word, for the simple reason that each of them was so boiling mad he couldn't speak. Finally, after they had showered and were climbing into their bunks, Tom spoke for the first time since leaving Vidac.

"I have to write a report to Captain Strong," he said, when Roger started to turn out the light. "Better leave it on a while, Roger."

"O.K., Tom," said Roger. "Are you going to tell him what's going on here?"

"Yeah," growled Astro. "Give him the whole works. There's something wrong here somewhere. I can understand the professor blasting his jets. He does that all the time. But I can't understand Vidac acting the way he does."

"I feel the same way, Astro," said Tom, "but actually what are we going to say to Captain Strong? So far nothing concrete has happened." He shook his head. "I'm afraid if I put what happened down on an audioscriber that it'll look as though we've suddenly become cry-babies!"

"I'm ready to quit!" said Roger. "Grab a freighter and blast outta here. A whole year with this guy! There's no telling what he's liable to do!"

Tom leaned over the table and stared at the bulkhead in front of him. He clenched his fists. Needless to say, he agreed with Roger, he had the same feelings. But he was powerless to do anything about it.

CHAPTER 7

"All set, Tom," called Roger, adjusting the valves that supplied a steady stream of oxygen into his space suit. Tom nodded and turned to Astro, seated behind them, his hand on the remote-control switch governing the huge air-lock portal on the jet-boat deck.

"Open her up, Astro," he ordered, his voice crackling through the spacephones inside his space helmet. Astro pressed the lever opening the sliding panel in the side of the hull of the *Polaris* and the cold blackness of outer space came into view.

Seated at the controls of the jet boat, Tom pressed down on the acceleration pedal, sending the tiny ship rocketing out of the *Polaris* like a projectile. As they circled their mother ship, Roger pointed out the vessel they were going to and Tom settled down to full throttle in the direction of Roald colony vessel Number Twelve. The huge converted luxury liner carrying many of the colonists was several lanes away in the sprawling formation of ships and it would take several minutes for them to traverse the four hundred miles to Number Twelve.

The three cadets were under orders to tour the fleet and observe conditions aboard the other ships. It was obviously a nuisance assignment since any extraordinary conditions could have been reported by teleceiver. But they were glad to get away from Vidac and Professor Sykes if only for a little while.

Holding the small vessel at full throttle, Tom settled back and pointed out several of the large star clusters in the clear airless void of space around them. Andromeda Galaxy whirled above them like a Fourth-of-July pin wheel. And the sun stars of Regulus, Sirius, and the Seven Sisters sparkled like diamonds on black velvet.

"Think we'll ever reach those babies?" mused Tom in a quiet voice.

"We're on the first step right now with this expedition," replied Astro.

"A short step," commented Roger. "To us Wolf 359 is a long way off, but when you stack it up against the distance to Regulus, for instance, it's just an inch."

"I'd sure like to go to Regulus," said Astro.

"So would I," snorted Roger. "But we'd probably wind up with a space crawler like Vidac for a skipper. That you can have!"

Nearing the first stop in their tour, Tom signaled ahead to Number Twelve to be taken aboard. He waited for the outer portal of the ship's air lock to be opened and then sent his tiny spacecraft into a shallow dive, applying his braking jets expertly to bring it to a dead stop inside the jet-boat deck of the converted space liner. The outer portal slid closed and a moment later the air pressure on the deck had been built up enough for them to remove their space helmets.

As they climbed out of the jet boat, the inner air-lock portal slid open and Tad Winters, the civilian captain of the liner, appeared. There was a scowl on his face and he made no attempt to hide his annoyance.

"Whose idea was this to come snooping around while we're in flight?" he snarled.

Astro bristled and stepped forward, towering over the smaller spaceman. "If we had anything to say about it, Mr. Winters, your company would be the last we'd want!"

Winters glanced at Tom and Roger who stood to one side silently, their faces grim.

Tom stepped forward. "Vidac sent us, Winters. We're here to check the departments and see that everything is in order."

"Vidac, eh?" sneered Winters. "What's the matter? Can't he do it himself, instead of sending a bunch of space squirts?"

"The lieutenant governor is busy," said Roger sarcastically. "Very busy, in fact."

"Doing what?" asked Winters.

"Trying to keep the rest of his space rats in line!" snapped Roger.

"Listen, you!" growled Winters, taking a threatening step toward Roger. "I don't have to take that from you. One word outta me, and Vidac'll bury you in the brig."

Tom quickly stepped between Roger and the angry civilian spaceman to prevent the impending fight. He stared at Winters and smiled. "What's the matter, Winters? Need Vidac's help in everything you do?"

"Aw, go blast your jets, you space-brained jerks!" snorted Winters. He turned back toward the hatch, but there was noticeably less swagger to his walk.

The three cadets smiled at each other and followed him into the main body of the ship.

While the *Polaris* was the command ship of the fleet, the nerve center of the entire operation, it was still hardly more than a prison ship for the cadets. In direct contrast, the space liner was bright, gay, and full of life. Everything imaginable for the convenience of the colonists had been installed aboard the massive ship. As the three cadets walked through the ship on their way to the control deck, they passed the auditorium where stereos were shown in the evenings and indoctrination lectures were given during the day. They passed a number of compartments that served as a school for the children of the colonists. There were workshops where the colonists could make objects for their future homes in their spare time. And in the heart of the ship was one of the most complete and extensive libraries in the Solar Alliance. Audioslides, soundscribers, story spools, question-and-answer tapes, everything designed to answer just about any question the human mind could ask.

The main living quarters of the ship were arranged so that each family had a small apartment, complete in every detail, to preserve as much of the family life as possible. There were no governors or supervisors to control the colonists. It had been decided to allow the colonists to choose their own leaders aboard the ships. But they were living together so peacefully, they hadn't found it necessary to select any one individual to be a leader. The ship was a miniature city.

As the Space Cadets made their rounds of the power deck, control deck, and radar deck, they were amazed by the excellence of the equipment and the care given it. And because they saw nothing to substantiate their suspicions of Vidac, and his hand-picked crew, on Number Twelve, they found themselves confused about their feelings toward him.

On the power deck, Astro had questioned a rocketman closely about the arrangement of the baffling around one of the firing chambers. The power-deck officer, Shilo Speed, heard Astro's questions, agreed with the cadet, and made the rocketman rearrange the baffling. Then, on the control deck, the pilot had been careless in maintaining his position with the other ships in the fleet. Tom mentioned it to Winters, and Winters immediately ordered the man off the bridge, and replaced him. Such action for the safety of the colonists had made the cadets wonder about Vidac's ability.

After inspecting the ship from radar mast to jet exhausts, the three cadets started back for the jet-boat deck. As they retraced their steps, they passed through the library and encountered Hyram Logan and his son Billy.

"Hello, Mr. Logan," greeted Tom with a big smile.

"Well, hello, Corbett," Logan replied. "Didn't know you were aboard Number Twelve."

"We're not assigned to her, sir," replied Tom. "We're just making an inspection for the lieutenant governor. How do you like the way she's being run?"

Logan's endorsement was immediate. "Just fine, Corbett. This ship is almost a colony in itself."

"Yeah, including school," chimed in Billy sourly. The three cadets laughed. Then the boy grinned and stuck a finger gently into Roger's stomach. "She ain't here, Cadet Manning. My sister is teaching kindergarten right now."

"Be quiet, Billy!" barked his father.

Roger's face turned a slow red while Tom and Astro grinned. After a few more words, the three cadets again headed for the jet-boat deck.

"That Billy will make a fine radarman someday," drawled Astro.

"How do you figure that, Astro?" asked Tom.

"Did you see the way he spotted Roger's roving eye looking for his pretty sister? Why, in ten years, he'll be picking up asteroids the same way."

Back in their jet boat a few minutes later, blasting through space on the rest of their tour, Tom turned to his unit mates, a troubled look on his face.

"Did you notice anything aboard Number Twelve that looked—well, suspicious?" he asked.

Astro and Roger shook their heads.

"Me neither," said Tom. "Maybe we've got Vidac pegged wrong. Maybe—"

"I thought of that, Tom," interrupted Roger. "But there's one thing that doesn't seem right."

"What's that?" asked Tom.

"Your report to Captain Strong," Roger replied. "You sent it to him ten days ago. You should have had an answer by now."

"He's out on Pluto," said Astro. "Space Academy might not have forwarded it to him."

"You know the rules," said Roger. "Any official communication to a Solar Guard officer is sent through regardless of where he is in the universe, if communications are at all possible."

"You're right, Roger," said Tom finally. "I should have had some sort of answer by now."

"You think," mused Astro slowly, "maybe Vidac didn't send the report?"

Roger hesitated and then replied, "There's one way to find out."

"How?" asked Tom.

"Take a look in the communications logbook on the control deck."

"We can't, Roger." Tom shook his head. "Vidac's got his own men planted in every one of our departments."

"Yeah," growled Astro. "I been watching the way that guy Smith takes care of the power deck and, believe me, it makes me burn. Why, he hasn't washed down the atomic motor casing once since we blasted off!"

"Wait a minute!" cried Roger suddenly. "Jeff Marshall!"

"Jeff?" asked Tom. "What about him?"

"He can get to the control deck and take a look at the logbook," answered Roger.

"Say, that's right," said Tom.

"Come on," said Roger. "Let's finish off this tour and get back to the *Polaris*. If Vidac's on the level, he'll have sent your report to Captain Strong. If not, we know where we stand."

Astro shook his head slowly. "Honestly, fellas, I don't know whether to hope he did or didn't."

* * * * *

Their tour completed, the three cadets returned to the *Polaris*. They quickly audioscribed their report to Vidac and then hurried to the observatory to find Jeff Marshall. Luckily the sergeant was alone and they were able to give him all the reasons for their suspicions of Vidac and tell him what they wanted him to do.

"But what can I say I'm looking for in the logbook?" Jeff Marshall protested.

"We passed through a cloud of meteor dust the other day, didn't we?" asked Tom.

"Yeah," replied Jeff, "but what's that got to do—"

"You had to report it to central weather control," said Tom. "Tell the pilot you lost your own copy of the report and want to get the official path out of the log. Tell him the professor wants it."

Jeff thought a moment, then nodded his head. "O.K. I'll see you later."

The three cadets returned to their quarters to wait while Jeff went up to the control deck. He walked in with a smile, chatted with the pilot a few moments, and then made his request.

"I want to take a look at the log a minute, Johnny," he said casually. "The professor lost his notes on the meteor dust we passed through the other day."

"Sure," said the pilot. He tossed the dog-eared book to the sergeant. Jeff flipped through the pages and found the day Tom's report was to have been sent. He checked carefully, continuing through the entries for the succeeding days, ending with the last entry made just an hour before. There was no mention of Tom's report. Jeff turned to give the logbook to the pilot when Vidac and Professor Sykes stepped through the hatch. Seeing Jeff with the log in his hands, Vidac frowned.

"What are you doing here, Marshall?" he snapped.

Jeff was trapped. He came to attention and remained silent. Vidac walked across the control deck and stood in front of him.

"Well, Marshall?" he barked. "Answer me!"

"I needed some information about the meteor dust we passed through recently, sir," said Jeff.

Vidac turned to the professor. "Did you send him up here?"

Sykes merely shook his head.

"I lost the professor's notes and needed the information in the logbook, sir," said Jeff.

"What are you talking about?" growled Sykes. "The notes are still in my work journal. You put them there yourself!"

"What have you got to say to that?" demanded Vidac.

"I repeat, sir," said Jeff, "that was my reason for looking in the log."

Vidac paused, and when he spoke, his voice was cold. "The control-deck logbook contains classified information, Marshall. You know that. I won't say you're lying about reasons for looking at it, but that does not excuse the fact that you *did* look at it without my permission. I'm confining you to the brig for ten days."

Jeff didn't bat an eyelash. The fact that he had found no entry of Tom's report to Captain Strong in the log, and the unreasonable annoyance Vidac expressed over his having looked into the logbook, convinced him that the cadets were not wrong in their suspicions concerning the lieutenant governor.

Vidac dismissed him and the enlisted sergeant was escorted to the *Polaris'* brig by two hastily summoned crewmen.

When the cadets learned of Jeff's punishment they immediately went to Vidac's quarters and requested permission to speak with him. After making them wait for nearly three hours, Vidac finally received them.

"Well, what now?" demanded Vidac.

"We would like to ask a question, sir," said Tom.

"Speak up!" snorted Vidac impatiently.

"It's about Sergeant Marshall, sir," said Tom.

"What about him?"

"We would like to know, sir, under what article of the space code was Sergeant Marshall sentenced to the brig?"

Vidac's eyes sharpened. He spoke quickly and crisply. "I suspected that there was some connection between Marshall looking in the log and your coming here to see me. I don't know what you have in mind, Corbett, but I'm going to lay it on the line. This is the last time you will question my authority. From this moment on, and until you are released from my jurisdiction, *I* am the space code. Do I make myself clear?"

"Very clear, sir," said Tom tightly. "Then will the lieutenant governor please put in writing any further orders he might have for us?"

"I will not!" snarled Vidac. "But I tell you what I will do. I'll confine you to your quarters for ten days for that impertinent request! And if I so much as see your noses outside your quarters, I'll really get tough! Dismissed!"

CHAPTER 8

"This is highly irregular, Logan," said Vidac to the Venusian farmer, "but I guess you can see the cadets. Perhaps a little advice from you will help them mend their ways."

Logan nodded. "I have a boy of my own, Governor," he said, "and I know how rambunctious they can get."

Vidac smiled thinly. "You'll find them in their quarters. The first ladder to your right and down two decks."

"Thank you, sir," replied Logan. He left Vidac's quarters and two minutes later stepped through the hatch leading into the cadet's room. After seven days of confinement, the three boys greeted Logan with a yell of pure joy.

"We have guests!" bellowed Astro, grabbing Roger who was asleep in his bunk and then banging on the shower door where Tom was taking a shower.

Roger tumbled out of the bunk and Tom came rushing out of the shower wrapped in a towel. They all began talking at once.

"How'd you know we were confined to quarters, sir?" asked Tom.

"It's a wonder Vidac allowed you to come see us!" yelled Roger.

"Never mind the questions, sir," said Astro. "It's just plain good to see a different face besides these two space jokers. One more game of space chess with Manning and I think I'd—"

Logan laughed at the cadets' enthusiasm, holding up both hands to stem their eager babbling questions. After Tom had dressed hastily and Roger had cleared off a bunk, they began to talk calmly.

"I didn't know you boys were in trouble," said Logan, "until I came over to the *Polaris* to see you. Then Vidac told me all about it."

"Was there any special reason why you wanted to see us, sir?" asked Tom.

"Well, as a matter of fact, there was a little reason. Billy, my son, has been pestering me to get some of your Academy books and audioscripts so he can study to become a Space Cadet when he gets old enough."

The three cadets grinned at each other and soon the Venusian farmer was piled high with manuals, audioscripts, tapes, and general information about the Academy.

"Thank you, boys," said Logan. "That's real nice of you, but—"

"But what, sir?" asked Tom.

"That was the little reason for coming to see you. I have a big reason too."

"What's that, sir?" asked Roger.

"I don't know how to say it exactly," began Logan, his voice low and hesitant, "but do you remember when you three came over to inspect Number Twelve?"

The boys all nodded and Logan continued in a hushed voice.

"Well, I told you then that everything was as nice as it could be. At that time it was. But now—"

"What's happened, sir?" asked Tom.

"What hasn't happened you mean!" snorted Logan. "The very next day we had a visit from Vidac himself. He made a routine check of all the departments, stopped and talked to some of the colonists, and he seemed, in general, like a nice fellow. Then all of a sudden it started."

"What?" asked Astro.

"Our skipper Winters and another fellow, Ed Bush, began treating us like—well, like prisoners!"

"Prisoners!" cried Tom.

"Yes!" said Logan. "They began to tell us when we couldn't go to the workshop and to the stereos, and made us eat our meals together in the main assembly room, with the wives taking turns doing all the cooking. And the schooling has been cut altogether."

"Why, why—" Tom was floored by the information. "But how can that be?"

"I don't know," said Logan, "but that's the way it is. I came over to tell you boys about it, since you were the only ones I knew. You struck me as being honest and I felt I could trust you."

"What else have Winters and Bush done?" asked Astro tensely.

"I guess the worst of all is the fact that we're having to pay for everything we eat," said Logan.

"Pay!" exclaimed Roger. "But, but—how can you? You don't have any credits. The Solar Council decided to let the colony work on a barter basis—share and share alike—until it could take its place in the over-all economy of the Solar Alliance."

"I know, I know," said Logan resignedly. "We're having to pay for the things we get by signing over a percentage of our future profit over the next seven years."

The three cadets looked at each other in disbelief. The idea of two men openly violating the laws of the expedition, treating the Solar Alliance citizens as if they were prisoners, was overwhelming.

Tom got up and began to pace the deck. Finally he turned and faced Logan. "Have you said anything to Vidac about this?" he asked.

"Ummmpf!" snorted Logan. "Every one of us signed a petition and had it sent to the governor himself. We didn't even get a reply. Vidac must have heard about it and told Winters and Bush to take it easy, because the next day we were allowed to eat again without having to sign over part of our profit to them. But everything else is the same."

"But how could they force you to pay?" asked Roger. "Couldn't you refuse?"

"Sonny," declared Logan emphatically, "I'm brave as the next man. But you don't argue against a paralo-ray gun, especially when there are women and children to worry about."

Tom whirled around and faced Roger and Astro. "I guess we don't need any more proof now," he said coldly. "Jeff Marshall is thrown into the brig for looking into a logbook; we're relieved of our jobs here on the *Polaris*; my monthly report to Captain Strong isn't sent to Space Academy, and now this. One of two things is happening. Either Governor Hardy is in on this with Vidac, or Vidac is taking over without Hardy knowing anything about it."

"All right—all right," growled Astro, "but what are we going to do about it?"

"We've got to get word to Space Academy or Captain Strong someway, somehow. We've got to let them know what's going on."

"There's only one way to do that," said Roger. "But with the communications controlled by Vidac's men, we don't have the chance of a snowball on the sunny side of Mercury!"

"Then," announced Tom firmly, "we'll have to build our own communications unit."

"But how?" asked Logan.

"Roger here can make a communicator out of spit and bailing wire," said Astro. "All he needs is the essential parts."

"Look," said Tom tensely, "Jeff Marshall will be getting out of the brig when we do. He'll be working with Professor Sykes, along with us. Why can't we build one on the sly in the observatory?"

Roger thought a moment. "It's the only thing we can do. I just hope that Mr. Logan's coming here hasn't aroused suspicion."

"Don't worry about that," said Logan. "I told Vidac I wanted this information about Space Academy for Billy. That seemed to satisfy him."

"I don't know," mused Tom. "He's pretty smart."

"What else can we do?" asked Astro.

"Nothing," said Tom bitterly. "Not a space-blasting thing until we get out of here!"

* * * * *

"We've *got* to have that triple vacuum tube," declared Roger. "That's the only thing that will transmit a voice quickly back to Earth from this fix out in space."

The three boys and Jeff Marshall were back in their quarters after their first week of active duty again. They had surreptitiously begun collecting parts for the communicator and were sorting them out on one of the bunks when Roger mentioned the necessity for the special vacuum tube.

"How quickly?" asked Astro.

Tom explained. "The equipment we have now is strong enough to talk to the Academy, but it'll take about six hours for my voice to reach it. And then another six hours for the Academy's answer to get back to us. At the end of twelve hours we might not be ready to receive and the communications officer might pick up their answer. Then we'd be in the middle of a space hurricane!"

"I see," said Astro. "You've got to be able to talk directly to the Academy, so that when they answer, you'll be ready!"

"Right," said Tom. "We might only get ten or fifteen minutes of free time, when the professor would be away from the observatory."

"Where do you think I could get one of those tubes, besides on the radar bridge, Roger?" asked Jeff. He had been the main source of supply for the equipment used in the communicator. Since getting out of the brig, his movements had not been as restricted as the cadets'.

"That's just it," said Roger. "I remember distinctly loading all of them in the locker near the main scanner on the radar deck."

"Then we have to get it from another ship," said Tom. "The chances of getting one here, aboard the *Polaris*, are zero."

"Say, Roger," suddenly asked Astro, "do you think you remember enough about that triple vacuum tube to draw me a blueprint?"

"Sure," said Roger. "And you could probably build it too. But how are you going to get the inside tube vacuumized, then the second one, and finally the third. They have to be absolutely clean!"

"How about outside in space?" Astro suggested. "We could take the parts of the tube with us and assemble it out there. You can't ask for a better vacuum than outer space."

Tom grinned and slapped the big Venusian on the back. "Astro, you're the hero of the day. Come on, Roger, start drawing that tube! Astro can make it on the power deck as if he were repairing something. Make it as simple as possible."

"Right," said Roger, "all I need is the vacuum and of course the copper filament inside the inner third tube for sending and receiving. We can make it so the tubes screw together inside of each other and then seal them."

"Right," said Astro.

"Meantime," said Tom, "Jeff and I will get you a set of earphones, if we have to tear them off the head of the radarman!"

Meanwhile, in Vidac's quarters, the second-in-command was facing the irascible Professor Sykes.

"Say that again, Professor," said Vidac. Sykes was standing before him holding a slip of paper in his hand.

"I said," the professor snorted, "that in forty-eight hours and some odd minutes we will be passing through a very thick cluster of asteroids, about ten thousand miles in depth."

"Is it on our present course?" asked Vidac.

"Yes," replied Sykes. "We'll have to go around it. I wouldn't give you a plugged credit for our chances of getting through it."

"I didn't ask you for your opinion!" snapped Vidac. "All right, you've given me your information. Now get out!"

Sykes abruptly turned and left the lieutenant governor's compartment. Alone, Vidac paced the floor. After a moment of deep thought he snapped his fingers in decision and turned on the ship's intercom.

"Corbett! Manning! Astro!" he bellowed. "Report to the control deck on the double."

A few moments later the three cadets stood before Vidac at rigid, stone-faced attention. Vidac turned on the chart projection screen and pointed to their position in space.

"Professor Sykes has just warned me that the fleet is approaching a freakish asteroid cluster," he announced. "He estimates it to be of this size." Vidac swept his arm over the chart, taking in most of the space directly in front of their path. "To go around it, over it, or under it would mean altering the course of the whole fleet and losing about six days' transit time." He turned back to the cadets who had been watching closely. "I want you three to see if you can find a route through the belt and save us the detour time." He glanced at his wrist chronograph. "The belt is about forty-one hours ahead of us now. Take a rocket scout, look it over, and report back to me."

"Yes, sir," said Tom. "Anything else, sir?"

"Yes," said Vidac. He stepped closer to the three boys. "This is not a joy ride. I expect you to find a way through that cluster. You have enough time to explore the greater part of it."

"But you said forty-one hours, sir," retorted Tom.

"That's plenty of time if you travel at full space speed."

"Full thrust!" exploded Roger. "In an unknown asteroid cluster? Why, the odds are better than a thousand to one that we'll be ripped open by a space rock. The best we can do is one-quarter space speed."

"You'll open those jets wide or you'll spend the rest of the trip to Roald in the brig and I'll send a report back to the Academy on your cowardice!" Vidac paused, then added quietly, "Do I make myself clear?"

"Yes, sir," said Tom, tight-lipped. "You make yourself perfectly clear!"

CHAPTER 9

"Do you think it will be safe there?" asked Roger, as he watched Tom and Astro push the half-completed communications set under a workbench behind several large cartons.

"As safe as any place," replied Tom. "If Vidac has any idea we're building it, we could hide it any place and he'd find it. So, as the saying goes, the least hidden is the best hidden. We'll have to take a chance."

"Besides," chimed in Astro, "here in the storeroom, Jeff will have his eye on it all the time. If Vidac starts getting nosy, Jeff will be able to shift it to another hiding place without too much trouble."

"Well, that's all we can do now," said Tom, straightening up. "Come on. Let's get to the scout ship and blast off before Vidac wants to know what we're doing."

Checking the hiding place one last time, the three cadets left the storeroom and headed for the jet-boat deck. In a few moments they were blasting through space toward the rear of the fleet where a rocket scout was waiting for them. The scouts were being carried by the larger space freighters to save fuel. Now one had been fueled and was blasting alongside its carrier ship with a skeleton crew. When the cadets' jet boat came alongside, the crew of the scout transferred into the jet boat and the three cadets took over the scout.

On the control deck, Tom checked his instruments and made preliminary tests on the circuits. Suddenly Roger's voice crackled over the ship's intercom. "Blast that guy Vidac!" he yelled. "He's one jump ahead of us again!"

Startled, Tom called into the intercom. "What do you mean, Roger?"

"The ship's communicator," snorted Roger. "I figured once we got aboard the scout we'd be able to use this set to contact the Academy instead of having to monkey around with the homemade job back on the *Polaris*. But it's no soap."

"Why not?" boomed Astro over the intercom.

"The only open circuit here is beamed to the *Polaris*. And the radar is too complicated to change over to audio communications. We haven't got enough time."

Tom clenched his teeth. He had had the same idea about using the communications set on the scout to contact the Academy. Now there was nothing to do but hope Vidac wouldn't find the one they were building. He called into the intercom again. "Is the radar working well enough for us to search the asteroid cluster without plowing into any space junk?"

"Yeah," growled Roger. "He left it in working condition all right, but if we burn out a tube, we're blacked out until we get back. There isn't a spare nut or bolt in the locker for repairs."

"But what happens if something happens to the radar when we're in the cluster," called Astro. "We'll be sitting ducks for every asteroid!"

"That's the chance we have to take, Astro," said Tom. "If we complained, you know what he'd do."

"I sure do," growled Astro. "He'd call us yellow again, because we'd refused to make the trip!"

"That's the way it adds up," said Tom. "So I guess we'd better get started. Stand by to blast!"

"All clear fore and aft," reported Roger.

"Full thrust, Astro," ordered Tom, "but stand by for emergency maneuvers. This is going to be a tough trip, fellows. Perhaps the toughest trip we've ever made. So keep your eyes and ears open and spaceman's luck!"

"Spaceman's luck!" echoed his unit mates.

Under full thrust the speedy little ship shot ahead of the fleet toward the gigantic mass of asteroids, planetoids, and millions of lesser space bodies, whirling and churning among themselves at an incredible rate of speed. Hardly had they left the fleet when Roger's voice crackled over the intercom again.

"Say, you space monkeys!" he yelled. "I got an idea! How about taking this wagon and heading back for the Academy?"

"Can't," replied Astro, "we've only got forty-eight hours of fuel, water, and oxygen—and no reserves. We couldn't get one-tenth of the way back before we ran out of everything, even if we wanted to go back."

"What do you mean—*if?*" snapped Roger. "Wouldn't you go back? How about you, Tom?"

"I'd think a long time before I would," said Tom. "Remember, Vidac hasn't done anything we can actually pin on him."

"What about making the colonists pay for their food," sneered Roger.

"Vidac could say it was a precautionary measure," said Tom.

"What kind of precaution?" asked Astro.

The speedy little ship shot ahead of the fleet toward the gigantic mass of asteroids

"Well, Vidac could say that the colonists were using too much of the supplies simply because it was free. And instead of imposing rationing, he's making them pay, but that he wouldn't actually take their profit."

"Yeah," growled Astro. "And there's just enough hokum in that to make everyone back at the Academy happy."

"I'm afraid we'll have to go on with it," said Tom. "Not only this exploration of the asteroid belt, but we'll have to wait for Vidac to really tip his hand."

"From the way he operates," said Roger disgustedly, "that might be never."

Blasting farther ahead through the unexplored region of outer space, the cadets, who had seen a great many space phenomena, were awed by the thickening groups of stars around them. It was Tom who finally realized that they were getting closer to the inner ring of their galaxy and that the stars and suns they were unable to see from Earth, or other Solar Alliance planets, were some fifty to sixty billion miles closer.

Gulping a cup of tea and a few sandwiches, the three cadets continued their advance toward the uncharted, unknown dangers of the asteroid belt that lay ahead of them.

Meanwhile, back on the *Polaris*, Jeff Marshall walked into the observatory quietly. He stood and watched Professor Sykes adjust the prisms of his telescopes, then settle himself to an hour of observation. Jeff knew that the professor would remain there for the next two hours. He felt safe in going to the storeroom and taking out the communications unit to work on it. But just to make sure, he called out, "Will you be needing anything, sir?"

"No, I won't!" barked Sykes. "If I did, I'd ask for it!"

"Yes, sir!" said Jeff. He turned away with a slight smile on his face and left the observatory. He walked quickly through the passageways of the ship until he came to the storeroom hatch. He glanced around quickly and then stepped into the quiet chamber. Pulling the cartons away from the bench, he took out the half-completed tangle of wires, and by the light of a small flashlight, he peered into the maze, trying to figure out where Roger had left off. He had traced the connections and was about to go to work when suddenly the overhead light was switched on, bathing the storeroom in light. Jeff whirled around to see Vidac, standing in the open hatch, staring at him.

"Well, Sergeant Marshall," he said, advancing toward the enlisted spaceman, "some secret experiment, no doubt!"

"Yes, sir," replied Jeff. "I've—I've been working on a new type of communications set."

Vidac stepped closer to the set and gave it a quick look. Suddenly, without warning, he picked up the delicate instrument, smashed it to the floor, and then trampled on it. He whirled around and faced Marshall.

"What's the meaning of this, Marshall?" he demanded.

Jeff was stunned by Vidac's violent action and could only stammer, "I have nothing to say, sir."

"Is Corbett or Manning or Astro in on this?" asked Vidac.

"No, sir," Marshall said quickly.

"I warn you, it won't go easy with you if I catch you shielding those cadets," snapped Vidac.

"No, sir," said Marshall, swallowing hard several times, "I am not shielding them."

"Very well, then. Tell me, what was the purpose of this 'experimental' communications set?"

"To make contact with amateur communicators back in our solar system, sir."

"I'll bet!" said Vidac coldly. "All right, pick up this piece of junk and get out of here. Any more experiments will take place in the observatory, and not unless I give my permission, is that clear?"

"Yes, sir," said Jeff. "I understand, sir."

Vidac turned and walked away without returning Jeff's salute. The enlisted spaceman looked down at the twisted mass of wire and metal and muttered a low oath. Then, picking up the pieces, he turned and walked wearily back to the observatory. All of Roger's effort was destroyed. But worse than that, now Vidac knew about the attempt to build the set.

* * * * *

"Watch out, Tom."

Roger's voice blasted through the intercom from the radar deck. "There's the biggest hunk of space junk I've ever seen bearing down on us!"

Tom flipped on the control-deck scanner of the rocket scout quickly, estimated range, angle, and approach of the onrushing asteroid, and called to Astro on the power deck.

"Emergency course change!" he bellowed. "One-quarter blast on the starboard jets, ten degrees down on the exhaust steering vanes! Execute!"

In the cramped space of the power deck, the giant Venusian quickly responded to his unit-mate's orders. Opening the induction valves leading to the reactors, the cadet shot full power into the radiation chambers, sending the little space scout into a long downward curve, safely out of the path of the dangerous asteroid.

"Whew!" breathed Roger over the intercom. "That was fast thinking, Tom. I wouldn't have had time to plot a course change. And with all that other stuff around here, we might have missed this one and hit two others!"

"Yeah," agreed Astro. "It must have been good, because I'm still here!"

"Got your radar sweeping ahead, Roger?" asked Tom. "Any sign of an opening in this stuff?"

"Radar's going all the time, Tom," replied Roger. "But I don't think we're going to find a passage large enough to take the whole fleet through."

"I'm afraid you're right," said Tom. "I guess we'd better get out of here. How much fuel do we have left, Astro?"

"Enough to hang around here for another fifteen minutes. But let's not cut it too fine. We might have to spend a little time looking for the fleet."

"I don't imagine Vidac would lose any sleep," sneered Roger, "if we got lost!"

"Well, fifteen minutes is fifteen minutes," said Tom, "so we might as well take a look."

Roger gave the course change to Tom and the small ship shot to another section of the asteroid cluster while the electronic finger of the radar probed ahead, searching for an opening through the mass of hurtling rock. Time and again in the past fifteen hours, the cadets had discovered what they thought to be a way through, only to find it too small for the massed flight of spaceships to maneuver safely. Now after the many hours of concentration the boys were tired and more than willing to return to the fleet.

"Time's up," Tom finally announced. "Plot a course back to the *Polaris*, Roger. Stand by for a course change, Astro. We're heading home!"

Tom's remark about heading "home" went unnoticed, since the three cadets had long since thought of the giant rocket cruiser as being their home, more than Space Academy or their real homes with their families.

After making contact with the *Polaris*, Roger quickly plotted an intersecting course that would put them alongside the command ship of the fleet in a few hours. Then, safely out of the dangerous cluster of flying meteors and asteroids, the three cadets gathered on the control deck and relaxed for the first time since the beginning of their scouting trip. They discussed their chances of contacting Space Academy with the communications set they had left hidden in the storeroom.

"How far did you get with the tube, Astro?" asked Roger.

"You'll be able to send out a message four hours after we get back," replied Astro between bites of sandwich.

"Too bad we don't have the tube with us," said Tom. "Now that we're alone we could vacuumize it without worrying about Vidac."

"I've already tried to make another one here," said Astro. "But these scouts don't have any kind of tools or equipment. We'll have to wait till we get back."

In a few hours Roger picked up the welcome outline of the *Polaris* on his scanner and, shortly after, the rest of the fleet. After receiving instructions from Vidac to return the scout to the freighter and come aboard, the three cadets made quick work of transferring to the jet boat and a short while later were waiting impatiently for the hiss of oxygen to fill the air lock of the *Polaris*. No sooner had the dial indicated the equal pressure with the rest of the ship than the inner portal opened to reveal Vidac waiting for them.

"Well?" he demanded at once. "Is there a way through the asteroid cluster?"

"No, sir," said Tom. "We searched practically the whole thing. There are a few openings, but none large enough to let the whole fleet through."

"I thought so," sneered Vidac. "You just blasted to the edge of the cluster and waited for enough time to pass and then came running back here!"

"Why, you—" growled Astro. He took a menacing step toward Vidac. The older spaceman didn't move.

"Yes, Cadet Astro?" said Vidac coldly. "Did you want to say something?"

Before Astro could speak, Tom stepped forward. "Regardless of what you may think, sir," he said, "we did search the belt and there wasn't any way through it."

"I have to accept your word, Corbett," said Vidac. He turned and started back down the companionway, then stopped and whirled around to face them again. "Incidentally, something happened while you were away. Jeff Marshall was found experimenting with a homemade communicator. Do you know anything about it?"

The three cadets were dumfounded. Finally Roger shook his head. "No—no, sir," he muttered. "We don't know anything about it."

Vidac smiled. "All right. That's all. Make out a full report on the scouting mission and send it to me immediately."

When the lieutenant governor had disappeared, Roger turned to face Tom and Astro. "Well, what do we do now?"

Tom answered between clenched teeth. "We're going to see Governor Hardy!"

CHAPTER 10

"Now, now, boys," purred Governor Hardy, "I think you're jumping to conclusions. Personally I'm very much pleased with the way Lieutenant Governor Vidac is handling details. And as far as the asteroid cluster is concerned, we'll go under it, or over it, or whatever is the shortest route."

"Yes, sir," said Tom, "but—"

"No *buts*, Corbett," said Hardy, still smiling. "This is a great undertaking and we need the co-operation of every member of the expedition. In a few days we'll be arriving at Roald and the strain of this long trip will be over. Mr. Vidac is a capable man and I trust him implicitly, no matter how strange his methods may appear. I urge you to bury any differences you might have with him and work for the success of the colony. Now what do you say?"

Tom glanced at his two unit mates. Roger shuffled his feet and looked down at the deck, while Astro studied the bulkhead behind the governor's desk. "If that's the way you want it, sir," said Tom, "then I guess we'll have to play along."

"I guess you will," said Hardy, a slight edge creeping into his voice. "And if you tell me any more wild, unsubstantiated stories such as Vidac sending you to scout an unknown asteroid cluster in a poorly equipped rocket scout—well, I'll have to take stronger measures to ensure your co-operation. Do I make myself clear?"

"Yes, sir," chorused the cadets. They saluted and left the room.

"Well," said Tom, when they had reached the safety of their quarters, "I guess that just about does it."

"Yeah. We played our last card," grumbled Roger. "Either Hardy is the smoothest crook in the world, or Vidac really has him space happy."

"I wouldn't bet that it isn't a little bit of both," commented Astro.

The hatch suddenly opened and the cadets spun around nervously.

"Jeff!" they yelled in unison.

"Hello, guys," said the enlisted man glumly as he entered the room. He slumped on Tom's bunk. "I've got bad news."

"We already know," said Roger. "Vidac met us before we got out of the air lock. He couldn't wait to tell us."

"He asked us if we knew anything about it," said Tom. "We told him No."

"I lied myself," said Marshall. "I—I was going to do a little work on it, hoping to have it ready for you when you got back, but—" He stopped and shrugged his shoulders.

"Never mind, Jeff," said Tom. "If Vidac suspected we were building that communicator, he'd have found it sooner or later. The thing is, what are we going to do now?"

"I'll tell you in three words," growled Astro. The others looked at the big cadet. "Sweat it out," he said finally.

Tom nodded his head. "You're right, Astro. We're tied hand and foot to this guy for the next eleven months."

"How about Governor Hardy?" suggested Jeff.

"We just saw the illustrious governor," said Roger bitterly. "And the only question left in our minds is whether Hardy is working for Vidac, or Vidac for Hardy. No one could be as blind to what's going on as Hardy seems to be."

"Three words," said Tom half to himself. "Sweat it out!"

* * * * *

Like a gleaming diamond on the black velvet of space, the sun star Wolf 359 loomed ahead of the giant fleet, solitary and alone in its magnificence. With the *Polaris* leading the way for the mass of space vessels that stretched back and away, the pioneers and their families blasted through the last million miles that separated them from their new home in deep space.

Fifty-five billion miles from their own sun, they were about to establish a colony as their forefathers had done centuries before them. Like the first colony in the new world, then on the Moon,

Mars, Venus, Mercury, Titan, and Ganymede, and hundreds of outposts in the asteroid belt, these Earthmen were braving new dangers and hardships, leaving the comfort of their homes to establish the first star colony. Inside each of the massive ships, Earthmen gathered around the scanners to look ahead across the abyss of space and gaze at their new home. Finally the momentous order came crackling through the teleceivers.

"*Polaris* to fleet! Single up for landing! Ships to follow the *Polaris* and touch down in order of their fleet numbers!"

On the control deck of the command ship, Vidac began barking orders to Tom. The three cadets had been reassigned to their original stations because of their intimate knowledge and sure handling of the giant ship.

"Prepare the ship for touchdown, Corbett!" yelled Vidac.

"Yes, sir," said Tom. He flipped on the intercom and barked orders to Astro below on the power deck.

"Stand by to reduce thrust to one-quarter space speed, Astro. Stand by forward nose braking rockets."

"Right," replied Astro.

"Hey, Roger!" yelled Tom. "How far are we from the surface?"

"Estimated distance to touchdown is two hundred thousand feet," answered Roger crisply.

"Reduce thrust to minimum, Astro," barked Tom, his eyes watching every dial and meter on the control board.

"Distance one hundred fifty thousand feet," reported Roger. "Looks like an open plain right below us. Maybe we'd better try for it, eh?"

"I guess so," said Tom. "Relay your scan down here to the control-deck scanner." Tom gave it a quick glance, saw that there was plenty of room on the plain Roger had mentioned to hold the entire fleet, and turned to Vidac. "Request permission to touch down, sir," said Tom.

"Granted," replied Vidac.

The curly-haired cadet turned back to the control board and once again checked his instruments. Behind him, Vidac and Governor Hardy watched the surface of Roald as the *Polaris* began to turn for her tailfirst landing.

"Cut all thrust at one hundred thousand feet, Astro," ordered Tom.

"Aye, aye," replied Astro.

"One hundred ten thousand feet," reported Roger. "One-O-seven, one-O-four, one hundred!"

Almost immediately, the blasting roar of the rockets was cut to a whisper and the ship began to drop toward the surface of the satellite.

Vidac jumped forward and grabbed Tom's shoulder. "What're you trying to do, Corbett? We're falling!"

"I have no data on the gravity of Roald," said Tom calmly. "The best way to find out is to check our rate of fall. I can then gauge the amount of braking power necessary."

Behind the two spacemen, Governor Hardy smiled. He stepped forward and tapped Vidac on the shoulder. "Whatever your difficulties coming out here with them, Paul, you've got to admit that they know how to handle this ship."

"Yeah," growled Vidac. "Too bad they don't know how to handle themselves as well."

Tom smarted under the sarcasm but concentrated on the task of getting the ship safely to the ground.

"Fifty thousand feet," reported Roger. "I'd say that the gravity of Roald is about 2.7 over Earth's, Tom."

"O.K., Roger," replied Tom. "Give her one-quarter thrust, Astro. We'll have to feel our way down."

As the rumble of the main rockets started again, Tom waited for the ship's descent to be checked, and sudden concern welled up within him as the ship failed to respond.

"Thirty-five thousand feet," reported Roger from the radar deck.

"Full thrust, Astro," called Tom, anxiously watching the approaching surface of Roald. He checked his instruments again and his heart jumped up into his throat. The needles of all the gauges and meters were dancing back and forth as though they were being flicked with invisible fingers.

Tom grabbed the intercom and shouted wildly. "Astro! Emergency space speed! We've got to get out of here!" Tom whirled around to face Vidac and Hardy. "You'd better call Professor Sykes up here, right away," he declared.

"Why? What's the matter?" stuttered Hardy.

"Something's interfering with our whole electrical system, sir," replied the cadet.

"What's that, Corbett?" snapped Sykes, stepping quickly through the hatch into the control room. Tom was about to repeat his statement when suddenly the rockets blasted loudly, and the ship tossed and rocked, throwing everyone off his feet. Astro had applied emergency power to his reactors, sending the *Polaris* hurtling back into the safety of space.

"By the rings of Saturn," bawled Sykes, after he had adjusted to the sudden acceleration, "I'll have that space-brained idiot court-martialed for this!"

"It's not his fault, Professor," said Hardy, getting to his feet again. "If Corbett hadn't ordered emergency space speed, we'd all be smeared across that plain down there." He pointed to the scanner screen where the surface of Roald could be seen receding rapidly.

"Umph!" snorted Sykes, "let me take a look at that control board."

Quickly and surely, the professor tested every major circuit in the giant panel. Finally he straightened up and turned to face Hardy.

"Governor," he said quietly, "I'm afraid you'll have to forget about landing on Roald until I can find the reason for the disturbance."

"Then it's not caused by any malfunction aboard the ship?" Vidac broke in.

Sykes shook his head. "Whatever force field caused those instruments to react the way they did came from Roald. You'll have to stand off until I can go down and make a complete investigation."

"Well, what do you think it is?" asked Hardy.

"It might be one of a hundred things," replied the professor. "But I wouldn't attempt to land down there until we know what's causing the interference and can counteract it."

"Space gas!" exploded Vidac. "Is this another of your tricks, Corbett?"

"Tricks, sir?" asked Tom stupidly, so incredible did the lieutenant governor's question seem.

"Yes, *tricks!*" roared Vidac. "Get out of the way. I can take this ship down." He sat down in the pilot's chair and called Roger on the radar bridge. "Notify all the other ships they are to stand off until we have made a secure touchdown!"

"Yes, sir!" replied Roger.

"Professor," whispered Tom, "do something!"

Sykes looked at Tom a moment and then turned to leave the control deck. He paused in the hatch to call back in a low voice, "What can you do with a madman?"

Helplessly, Tom turned to appeal to Governor Hardy but changed his mind and stood beside Hardy, crossing his fingers.

At the controls Vidac gripped the acceleration lever and called into the intercom, "Stand by for touchdown. Power deck, cut all thrust!"

"Power deck, aye, sir," reported Astro.

As the main rockets were cut out again and the *Polaris* slipped back through space toward the surface of Roald once more, Tom stood behind Vidac with Hardy and watched the instruments begin their strange gyrations again. The cadet glanced at Hardy, whose face was impassive.

"Sir," asked Tom quietly, "isn't there something we can do?"

"Keep quiet, Corbett," snapped Hardy. "That's what you can do!"

"Yes, sir," replied Tom. He turned away to climb into the nearest acceleration chair and strap himself in. He knew it was possible for the *Polaris* to land successfully. He felt sure he could have made a touchdown on the satellite without trouble, but his first thought had been for the safety of the others aboard the ship. Now it was out of his hands and he grudgingly admired the way Vidac was handling the giant rocket cruiser.

"Twenty-five thousand feet to touchdown," reported Roger.

So far, Vidac had kept the ship dropping at a steadily decreasing rate. But the tension on the control deck mounted as the surface of Roald loomed closer and closer.

"Fifteen thousand feet," reported Roger.

Governor Hardy walked to a near-by acceleration chair and strapped himself in.

"Ten thousand feet!" yelled Roger.

"Power deck, give me three-quarters thrust!" ordered Vidac. Tom heard the whine of the rockets on the power deck increase with a sharp surge.

"Seven thousand feet," reported Roger.

Vidac remained cool, staring at the control board. Tom wondered what it was he was watching, since there wasn't one instrument that registered properly.

"Five thousand feet!" screamed Roger. "Spaceman's luck!"

The Polaris *landed safely on the surface of the satellite*

Immediately Vidac ordered Astro to apply full thrust to the main rockets. The great ship bucked under the sudden acceleration, and Tom could feel the tug of war between the cruiser's thrust and the satellite's gravity. The ship continued to drop at slightly lessened speed, but still too fast to land safely.

Tom waited for Vidac to order emergency thrust to counter the pull of the satellite. They were dropping too fast. He watched Vidac and waited for the only order that would save the ship. If he doesn't do it now, thought Tom, it will be too late.

"Vidac!" yelled Tom. "Emergency power! We're falling too fast!"

Vidac didn't answer. "Vidac!" screamed Tom again. "Emergency power!"

The man didn't move. He sat in front of the control panel as though paralyzed. Tom slipped off the straps of the acceleration chair and raced to the intercom. Vidac made no attempt to stop him.

"Astro! Full emergency thrust! Hit it!"

In immediate reply, a jolting burst of power blasted through the tubes, jerking the ship convulsively and throwing Tom to the deck. A loud, crashing sound filled the ship, followed by a strange stillness. Dimly Tom realized that the rockets had been cut and they were safely on the surface of the satellite.

He picked himself up and turned to face Vidac. The lieutenant governor was unstrapping himself from the pilot's chair. His face was ashen. He stalked out of the control deck without a word.

"Touchdown!" screamed Roger from the radar deck. "We made it. We're on Roald!"

Tom heard the blond-haired cadet, but his unit mate's excitement did not register. He was staring at the open hatch. "He lost his nerve," said Tom aloud, half to himself and half to Governor Hardy who was unstrapping himself from the acceleration chair. "He quit cold!"

"He certainly did," said Hardy. "And if it wasn't for your quick thinking, we'd be spread all over this satellite!"

Roger tumbled down the ladder from the radar deck. "Nice work, Tom," he shouted, slapping his unit mate on the back. He followed Tom's gaze past Hardy to the empty hatch.

"Say, can you imagine a guy like that suddenly losing his nerve?" asked Roger.

"No," replied Tom. "If I hadn't seen it with my own eyes I wouldn't believe it!"

"This will go on your official record of course," said Hardy. "I'll see that you're rewarded in some way, Corbett."

"Thank you, sir," said Tom. "But if you could just assure me that my reports back to the Academy will get through, I'll be very happy."

"You mean they're not being sent?" asked Hardy, seemingly quite concerned.

"No, sir," replied Tom. "At least I don't think so. And this is the first time I've had a chance to tell you."

"Well," said Hardy, "there's a lot to be done now that we've arrived, Corbett. I'll take this matter up with Vidac as soon as I get a chance." He turned and walked off the control deck.

"Well, I'll be a space monkey!" exclaimed Roger.

"Yeah," agreed Tom, "I'll be two of them!"

CHAPTER 11

"Of the thousand ships that blasted off from Earth there are only six hundred thirteen left that can be used in the construction of the first colony of Roald."

Governor Hardy's voice was firm as he addressed the assembled colonists and spacemen from the air lock of a space freighter.

There was a murmur among the colonists at this news. They knew that the landings on the satellite had been costly; that many ships had crashed as a result of the unexplained interference with the ships' instruments. And since each ship had been designed to be cannibalized into houses, workshops, and power plants, they realized the plans for the settlement would have to be radically revised.

Once the *Polaris* had landed safely, the other ships of the fleet had followed, each trying to find the delicate balance between the pull of the satellite and the thrust of their rockets. And since many of Vidac's hand-picked crewmen were in control, a large number of the valuable and irreplaceable ships and their supplies had been lost. They didn't burn when they crashed. Fire could have been easily extinguished. Instead, deadly radiation from the cracked firing chambers flooded the ships and their cargo, rendering them useless.

Tom, Roger, and Astro stood with Jeff Marshall and the Logan family as the governor outlined their initial objectives on the satellite.

"First," declared Hardy, "we have to build atmosphere booster stations. We can't live without oxygen and there isn't enough oxygen in the atmosphere to sustain us very long. Second, we have to establish our ownership boundaries and begin planting our crops. We can't live without food. Third, we have to live more frugally than ever before in order to maintain our reserves of food and essential items. The nearest supply center is fifty billion miles from here." He paused and surveyed the sea of grim faces before him.

"We've had a hard blow," he continued, "in losing so many ships and their supplies, but it will not defeat us. We all came here with the understanding that it would be difficult. We did not expect an easy life. We knew it would be tough, but not quite as tough as it's going to be now. But we will win! And remember, we are no longer people of Venus, Earth, Mars, or Titan, we are citizens of Roald!"

There was a roar of approval from the colonists. A band began to play and the assembly was adjourned.

"He talks sense," Hyram Logan commented. "Real fighting sense!"

"I'd like it a lot better, though," replied Astro, "if he didn't make it sound like a rally."

"Yeah," agreed Roger. "He sounded as though he was pepping up his team to do or die in a mercuryball game."

"This is no game," said Tom. "We're fighting starvation, perhaps death! And, believe me, if this colony goes the way of all space dust, it will be a long time before there'll be another fleet of a thousand ships gambled on a star colony!"

Logan nodded his head. "That's the way I look at it, Tom," he said. "Regardless of what kind of beef we might have with Hardy or Vidac and his crew, we all have to work together to make Roald a colony. A successful colony!"

Returning to Fleet Ship Number Twelve, which was to be used for quarters by the colonists until their homes could be erected, the three cadets and Jeff Marshall said good-by to the Venusian farmer and continued on toward the *Polaris*.

"Did Professor Sykes find any indication of what might have caused the instruments to act up during the landing, Jeff?" asked Tom. The curly-haired cadet referred to the professor's investigation started as soon as the *Polaris* had landed.

"Nothing so far, Tom," replied Jeff. "But it must be something big. He packed a lot of gear into a jet boat and blasted out of here this morning."

"What do you suppose it is?" asked Astro.

"I don't know," replied Jeff. "I can't even guess."

"I can," said Roger, "and if it's what I think it is—well, I just hope it isn't, that's all." The blond-haired cadet stopped talking abruptly.

Tom, Astro, and Jeff looked at each other. Finally Tom asked, "Well, what do you think it is?"

"There's only one thing I know really well, Tom," replied Roger. "Just one thing, and that's electronics. I may be a jerk about a lot of things, but I know electronics."

"O.K.," said Astro. "You know electronics. But what has that got to do with the instruments going out of whack?"

"The only natural element that would cause such disturbance is uranium."

"Uranium!" breathed Tom. "You mean uranium pitchblende?"

"I mean uranium!" snapped Roger. "Uranium pitchblende isn't concentrated enough to cause a reaction like that on the instruments. It would take a big chunk of pure uranium to do the job."

"But if that were so," Astro protested, "wouldn't the instruments still be acting up? In fact, wouldn't we start feeling the effects of the radiation?"

"Not necessarily, Astro," said Tom. "I understand what Roger's getting at. The uranium could be located in another sector of the satellite, on the other side, maybe. It could be throwing radiation out into space without affecting us here."

"You mean we're *under* the effects?" asked Astro.

"Looks like it," replied Tom. "But on the other hand," he continued, "why wasn't there some report of it when the first expedition came out to look over the satellite?"

"I can't answer that question, Tom," answered Roger. "But I'd be willing to bet my last credit that there's uranium on this space-forsaken rock. And a whopping big deposit of it!"

They reached the air lock of the *Polaris* and climbed wearily aboard. At the end of the first day, on the new satellite, they were exhausted. A few minutes after entering the giant cruiser they were all sound asleep.

Dawn of the second day on Roald saw the vast plain crowded with men at work. The first community objective was the construction of an atmosphere station, and before the woman and children had finished lunch, they were breathing synthetically produced air.

Working from a master plan that had been devised back at Space Academy before the expedition blasted off, the colonists were divided into three separate crews: the wreckers, those who would remove essential parts from the spaceships as they were needed; the movers, those who would haul the parts to construction sites; and the builders, those who would take the parts and construct the community buildings.

The first and most difficult job was building a gigantic maneuverable derrick and jet barge for removing, hauling, and installing the heavy machinery.

Astro had been assigned to the crew responsible for the construction of the jet barge. With many of the vital parts aboard the crashed freighters still hot with radioactivity, the crew had to improvise. And Astro, with his native talent for mechanics, soon became the unspoken leader of the crew. Even the supervisor acknowledged the young cadet's superior ability and allowed him a free hand in the construction of the barge. After six hours of hard labor, the "mover" was finished. It was not the streamlined machine its designer had conceived, but it was effective, in some cases, more so than the designer imagined. A low, flat table roughly three hundred feet square, it moved on sledlike runners and was powered by two dozen rockets. On each of the four sides there was a two-hundred-foot boom which could be swung around in a 360 deg. arc and was capable of lifting three hundred tons. Astro's most outstanding improvement on the original design was what he termed "adjustment rockets," placing single rockets that could be individually controlled on all four sides, so that the operator of the giant jet barge could jockey into perfect position anywhere. The machine quickly demonstrated it could move anything, anywhere.

Roger worked with the supervisor of the assembly groups, ordering supplies and machinery as they were needed from the wrecking crews and seeing that they were sent to the right place at the right time. One of his first jobs was the assembling of materials for the construction of the Administration Building of the colony. Less than five days after the foundation had been dug, the last gleaming sheets of Titan crystal were welded together and the building towered over the plain, a glistening monument to man's first flight to the stars.

Tom had been assigned to work closely with Vidac, who was responsible for all the construction on Roald. The young cadet welcomed the chance to observe the man in action, and time after time he found contradictions in the character of the lieutenant governor. Vidac's attitude and behavior in his drive to build the colony were completely different from his actions on the long space flight. He was a man of firmness and immediate decision. Shooting from one project to another in a jet boat, he would listen to the supervisors' complaints, make a snap decision, and then head for another project. Once Tad Winters and Ed Bush, who had taken over Astro's jet barge, had hesitated when trying to transfer a four-hundred-ton lift. A bank of atomic motors from Fleet Ship Number Twelve was to be installed in the main power plant for the colony. The motors were in a position where it was impossible to use more than one of the booms for the lift. Bush and Winters tried futilely to maneuver the jet barge into position where they could use two booms, and when Vidac arrived he promptly took charge. Using Tom as signalman, Vidac stood at the controls of the giant derrick, and after testing the strain on the five-inch cables, he yelled down to the cadet:

"Think they'll hold, Corbett?"

Tom looked at the derrick, the motors, and the boom Astro had constructed. Finally he nodded his head. If anyone else had built the jet barge, Tom would have said No, but he knew when the Venusian built something it was built solidly.

Stepping back out of range, Tom watched Vidac slowly apply power to the rockets on the jet barge. Slowly, inch by inch, the boom began to bend under the load. Vidac continued to apply power. The boom bent even more and still the motors would not lift free of the ground. The rocket exhausts on the jet barge glowed fiery red under the sustained surge of power. All over the colony, men stopped work to see if the jet barge would handle the outsized lift.

Vidac sat at the controls calmly and watched Tom. The curly-haired cadet continued to wave his hand to lift the motors. The boom continued to bend, and just as Tom thought it must snap, the motors lifted free and Vidac swung them around to the table top of the barge. He climbed down and walked over to Bush and Winters.

"Next time you're afraid to try something and waste valuable time," he barked, "you'll pay for it!"

He turned to Tom. "Let's go, Corbett," he said casually.

Day after day the work continued and finally, at the end of three weeks, the dry barren plain had been transformed into a small city. Towering above the city, the Administration Building glistened in the light of their new sun, Wolf 359, and streets named after the colonists radiated from it in all directions, like the spokes of a giant wheel.

There were houses, stores, and off the central square a magnificent assembly hall that could be transformed into a gymnasium. There were smaller community buildings for sanitation, water, power, and all vital services necessary to a community. Along the wide spacious streets, still being paved, converted jet boats hummed. Women began to shop. Men who had helped build the city the day before, now appeared in aprons and began keeping account books until a monetary system could be devised. A medical exchange that also happened to sell spaceburgers and Martian water was dubbed the "Space Dump" and crowds of teen-agers were already flocking in to dance and frolic. A pattern of living began to take form out of the dead dust of the star satellite. Several of the colonists who had lost everything aboard the crashed ships were made civilian officials in charge of the water, sanitation, and power departments.

The three cadets worked harder than they had ever worked before. Once, when the jet barge needed to be refueled, Vidac had ordered them to salvage the remaining reactant from the crashed ships and they worked forty-eight hours in lead-lined suits transferring the reactant fuel to the jet barge.

In addition, Roger was now hard at work building a communications center and a network all over the satellite. Communicators were placed at intervals of ten miles, so that any stranded colonist was within walking distance of help.

The four hundred ships that had crashed had been loaded mostly with farming equipment, and the seriousness of the situation was discussed at great length by Logan and other farmer colonists. Vidac had tried to salvage some of the more basic tools needed in farming the dusty satellite soil, but nothing had come of it. Three to five years had to pass before the radioactivity would be harmless.

"We'll have to farm with chemicals," announced Vidac finally to a meeting of the farmers. "I know that chemical crops are not as tasteful as naturals, but they are larger, more abundant, and nourishing." He paused and looked at the men. "However, even chemicals are not the whole answer."

"Well," said Hyram Logan, who had become the unofficial spokesman for the farmers, "give us the chemicals and let's get to work. Everyone here knows how to grow crops out of a test tube!"

"I'm afraid it won't be as simple as that," said Vidac. "Perhaps you remember that you paid over part of your future profits during the trip out from Atom City?"

There was a murmur from the group of men as the outrageous incident was brought up. Most of the men felt that Vidac had been directly responsible. Vidac held up his hand.

"Quiet, please!"

The men became silent.

"You will have to purchase the necessary material for farming from me. You will sign over one-half of your future profits to the treasurer of the Roald City Fund, or you don't farm."

"What's the Roald City Fund?" demanded Isaac Tupin, a short, thin man with an uncanny knack for farming. He had been very successful on Mars and had been asked to institute his methods of desert farming on the dusty satellite.

"The Roald City Fund," said Vidac coldly, "is an organization dedicated to the good and welfare of the citizens of Roald."

"Who's the treasurer?" asked Logan.

"I am," said Vidac. "Governor Hardy is now in the process of setting up Roald currency. Each of you will be allowed to borrow against future yields, a maximum amount of five thousand Roald credits. This will be your beginning. If your crops fail"—Vidac shrugged his shoulders—"you will forfeit your land holdings!"

There was a storm of protest from the assembled farmers. They stood up in their chairs and hooted and howled. Vidac faced them coldly. At last they fell silent and Vidac was able to speak again.

"I would advise you to consider carefully the proposal I've made here. Your equipment—the equipment given to you by the Solar Alliance—has been lost. The chemicals which you are now being offered are the property of the official governing body of Roald. We cannot give you the material. We can loan it to you, providing that you guarantee the loan with your future profits. All those interested may draw the necessary supplies from Tad Winters and Ed Bush in the morning."

He turned and walked out of the hall.

"We'll go to the governor!" shouted Logan. "We won't be treated like this. We're free citizens of the Solar Alliance and under their jurisdiction. We know our rights!"

Suddenly Tad Winters and Ed Bush appeared, seemingly from nowhere. A sneering smile on his face, Winters held two paralo-ray guns and covered the group of farmers while Bush slipped up behind Logan and hit him on the back of the neck. The elderly man sank to the floor.

"Now get this!" snarled Winters to the colonists. "The joy ride is over! You take orders, or else!"

CHAPTER 12

"What do you want?" growled Ed Bush. He stood at the air lock of the *Polaris*, a brace of paralo-ray guns strapped to his side. "Why ain't you out growing corn?"

Hyram Logan smiled. He held out the books and study spools the cadets had given him on the trip out. "I wanted to return these to the cadets. They lent them to my son. He wants to be a Space Cadet when he's old enough."

"I can think of a lot better things he could be," sneered Bush. He jerked his thumb toward the entrance port of the giant spaceship. "All right, get aboard. You got a half-hour."

Logan entered the cruiser quickly and made his way to the cadets' quarters. Tom was asleep. Roger and Astro were playing a game of checkers. When Logan entered, the two cadets quickly forgot their game and turned to greet the farmer.

"Hiya, Mr. Logan!" said Astro. "You saved me from doing a wicked deed."

Logan stared at the big cadet, puzzled. "How's that again, Astro?"

Roger laughed. "He's joking, sir. I was about to clean him out in a game of checkers."

Logan sat wearily on the side of the nearest bunk. "I wish all I had to lose was a game of checkers."

He quickly filled in the details of the meeting between Vidac and the farmers. Tom had awakened by this time and heard the last of the older man's story. He turned to his unit mates.

"Well, it looks as though we're right back where we started," he said. "And here I thought Vidac was O.K. after the way he worked during the past ten days setting up Roald City."

"I've been talking to some of the other men," said Logan bitterly. "They feel the same way I do. Something's got to be done about this!"

"But what?" asked Roger.

"And how?" chimed in Astro.

"Force, by the stars!" yelled Logan. "And when I say force, I mean throwing Vidac and Hardy and his crew out!"

"You can't do a thing like that, sir," said Tom. "It would be playing right into their hands. Remember, Vidac and Hardy represent the Solar Alliance here on Roald. If you tried force, you would be charged with rebellion against the Solar Alliance!"

"Well," snorted Logan, "what have *you* got in mind?"

"When the enemy is in full control, Mr. Logan," said Tom quietly, "the best thing to do is draw back and regroup, then wait for the right moment to attack. Vidac wants you to revolt now. He's expecting it, I'm sure. But if we wait, he can't get away with making you mortgage your land holdings or your profits. Somewhere along the line he'll slip up, and when he does, that's when we start operating!"

Meanwhile, in his luxurious office in the Administration Building, Vidac sat behind a massive desk, talking to Tad Winters.

"Now that the land boundaries have been established, and the colonists have their little pieces of dirt," he said, "we can go right to work. I've told the farmers that they'll have to sign over half of their profits to get chemicals to farm with. They're already talking about revolt, which is just what I want them to do. Let them rebel. We can throw them into the brig, send them back to Earth, and take over their property in the name of the City of Roald!"

"Which is you," said Tad Winters with a smile. "That's the smartest idea you've ever had, boss!"

"In a short while," continued Vidac, "the entire satellite will be mine. Ships, houses—and—"

Suddenly the door opened and Ed Bush hurried into the room. "Boss!—boss!" he shouted breathlessly. "Logan is spilling everything to the Space Cadets!"

"What?" cried Vidac. "How did that happen?"

"He came to the *Polaris*," whined Bush. "Said he had some books and stuff he wanted to return, so I let him aboard. Luckily I followed him and listened outside the door."

"What did they talk about?" demanded Vidac.

"Logan told them about the meeting with the farmers the other night. He wanted to get the colonists together to start a rebellion, but Corbett convinced him it would be the wrong thing to do."

"What?" yelled Vidac. He rose and grabbed Bush around the throat. "You dirty space crawler! You've ruined everything. All my plans messed up, because you let a hick and a kid outsmart you!"

"I'm sorry, boss," Bush whined. "I didn't know."

"Get out of here!" Vidac snarled. "I should have known better than to jeopardize the whole operation by signing on a couple of space jerks like you two! Get out!"

The two men left hurriedly and Vidac began to pace the floor. He was acutely aware that his scheme was out in the open. All of the careful planning to keep the cadets off balance and unsure of him until he could make his move was lost. He regretted not having gotten rid of them before, out in space, where unexplained accidents would be accepted. He had placed too much confidence in Bush and Winters and had underestimated the cadets. Something had to be done—and fast! But it couldn't be anything obvious, or his plans of taking over Roald would fail.

The buzz of the teleceiver on his desk interrupted his train of thought and he flipped open the small scanner.

"Professor Sykes to see you, sir," reported his aide in the outer office.

"Tell him to come back later," said Vidac. "I'm busy."

"He says it's very important," replied the aide.

"All right—all right, send him in," snapped Vidac and closed the key on the teleceiver irritably. A second later the door opened and Professor Sykes entered hurriedly. He was dirty and dusty from his ten-day stay in the desert wastes of the satellite.

"Vidac!" cried Sykes excitedly. "I've just made the most tremendous discovery in the history of the Solar Alliance!"

Vidac eyed the professor calculatingly. He had never seen the old man excited before. "Sit down, Professor," he said. "You look as if you just walked through the New Sahara on Mars. Here, drink this!" Vidac offered the professor a glass of water and waited expectantly.

Sykes drank the water in one gulp and poured another glass before taking his seat. He began digging into his pouch and pulling out sheets of what appeared to be exposed film. He rummaged around for his glasses, and after adjusting them on his hawklike nose, began to sort the sheets of film.

"When the instruments on the *Polaris* went crazy out in space," began Sykes nervously, "I knew there was only one thing that could cause such a disturbance. Radioactivity! As soon as we landed, I began to look for the source. At first I used a Geiger counter. But I couldn't get an accurate count. The counter was as erratic as the instruments. So I tried film. Here is the result." He handed the exposed film to Vidac. "This film was protected by lead sheeting. It would take a deposit of pitchblende richer than anything I've ever heard of to penetrate the lead. But look at it! The film is completely exposed. The only thing that could do that is a deposit of uranium at least seventy-five per cent pure!"

Vidac studied the films closely. "Where is this strike?" he asked casually. "Is it on land that has been parceled out to the colonists?"

"I don't know whose land it's on. But I'm telling you this! It's going to make someone the richest man in the Solar Alliance!"

Sykes fumbled in his pouch again and this time brought out a dirty piece of paper. "This is a report giving the location and an assay estimate. It has to be sent back to the Solar Council right away. Have communications with Earth been established yet?"

Vidac shook his head and reached out for the report. "If what you say is true," he said coolly, "we can always send it back on the *Polaris*."

He took the report and read it over. He recognized immediately the danger of Sykes's discovery. He laid the film and the report on his desk and faced the professor. "And you are absolutely sure of your findings?"

Sykes snorted. "I've been working with uranium all my life. And I should know a deposit like this when I see one!"

Vidac didn't answer. He turned to the teleceiver and flipped it on. "Send Winters and Bush in here right away," he told the aide.

"You going to send those two back with this report?" asked Sykes. "Personally I'd feel a lot safer if you'd send those Space Cadets and my assistant, Jeff Marshall. They may be young, but they can be depended on."

"I'd rather send men *I* can depend on, Professor," said Vidac. "As you say, the cadets are still quite young. And this report is too important to take chances."

The door opened and Winters and Bush entered.

Vidac stuffed the report and the exposed film into a dispatch case and quickly sealed it. He handed it over to Winters. "Guard this with your life," said Vidac seriously.

"Wait a minute," said Sykes. "Aren't you going to tell Governor Hardy about this?"

"This is so important, Professor," said Vidac, "that I think we should get it off at once. There's plenty of time to tell the governor."

"Well, all right." Sykes got up and stretched. "After almost two weeks in that desert, I'm ready for a nice clean bed and something to eat besides synthetics." He turned to Winters and Bush. "That pouch is worth more than any man ever dreamed of. Be sure you guard it well!"

"You can depend on us, Professor," said Winters.

"Yeah," said Bush. "Don't worry about a thing."

The three spacemen watched the professor leave. As soon as the door closed, Vidac grabbed the pouch out of Winters' hand. His face hardened and his eyes were narrow slits.

"You messed up one operation for me, but luck has given us another chance. If you mess this one up, I'll dump you into space for a long swim. Now listen to me!"

The two spacemen crowded close to Vidac's desk.

"Sykes has just made the biggest discovery in the universe. It's worth billions! The cadets are in our way, and as long as the professor is alive, so is he! We're going to wipe them out. I want you to take the professor to that asteroid we spotted a few days ago and keep him there. I'm going to accuse the cadets of getting rid of the old man, so we can eliminate the cadets, the professor, and keep the uranium secret for ourselves. His report says it's located at section three, map eight. That's the property given to Logan. After we get rid of the cadets and the professor, we'll have plenty of time to bounce old Logan. This is the sweetest operation this side of paradise. And it's all mine!"

"But what kind of proof will you have that the cadets did something to the old man?" asked Winters. "Getting rid of Space Cadets is a pretty tricky job."

"Tomorrow I'll assign the cadets to work with the professor again. That jerk, Manning, has a sharp tongue. I'll set up something that will get them into an argument in the presence of some of the colonists. When Sykes disappears right after that, we'll have witnesses to prove that Manning was gunning for the old man!"

"But how do you know that Manning will get mad enough?" asked Bush.

Vidac smiled. "I know Manning. And besides, I know what I'm going to do, to *make* Manning blast his tubes!"

CHAPTER 13

The first real community problem came when it was learned that the entire supply of school study spools were lost in the crashed ships. There was talk among the colonists of sending a ship back to Earth at once for replacements, but Vidac stepped in and took over. He called a meeting with the three Space Cadets, Jeff Marshall, and Professor Sykes, and told them of his plan.

"I want you to make new study spools on every subject you can remember," Vidac ordered. "Simple arithmetic, spelling, geography, celestial studies, physics, in fact, everything that you learned in prep school—and before that."

"That may be all right for boys," grumbled Professor Sykes, still smarting under the refusal of his violent protest at being taken from his uranium studies and placed in charge of the school problem. "But what about the girls? There are quite a few of them and they need special consideration."

"What kind of consideration?" asked Vidac.

"Well, whatever it is a girl has to know. Sew, cook, keep house, take care of children and—and—" The professor sputtered, hesitated, and concluded lamely, "A—a lot of things!"

Vidac smiled. "Very well. I'll speak to a few of the mothers and see if I can't get you some assistance. In the meantime, I want you, Corbett, Manning, Astro, and Marshall to do what you can about beginning the children's schooling."

"All right," snorted Sykes, "but I can think of better ways to spend the next two or three weeks."

"And one more thing, Professor," continued Vidac. "I want it clearly understood that you are responsible for the cadets. For what they do, or *don't* do!"

The faces of the three cadets began to flush under the sarcasm.

"And I want you to pay particular attention to Manning," Vidac went on. "He seems to have the biggest mouth in the unit."

"Well, he'd better watch his step with me or he'll find himself in a space hurricane!" Sykes said gruffly.

Vidac turned to Roger, but the blond-haired cadet was staring down at his boots. Vidac suppressed a smile. A few days under the whiplash tongue of Sykes, who would be anxious to finish the project and return to his own studies, and Manning would either buckle or flare up in open revolt. The lieutenant governor considered the possibilities and nodded in satisfaction.

"That's all, Professor Sykes," he said, rising and then turning to the cadets. "And I'd advise you boys to give the professor all the aid you can."

"Yes, sir," said Tom. "We understand. We'll do our best."

"Dismissed," said Vidac.

The three cadets and Marshall saluted sharply and filed out of the room. But Professor Sykes hesitated and turned to Vidac.

"I'd like to speak to you a moment about the—ah—"

"That's been taken care of, Professor," replied Vidac. "Nothing to worry about."

"Has the complete report been sent back?" asked Sykes.

"I said it had been taken care of," answered Vidac coolly. "That's all you have to know! Dismissed!"

Sykes hesitated, nodded, and finally followed the cadets from the room.

Vidac turned and flipped on the intercom. "I want Ed Bush in here and I want him fast!" he barked. Then, swinging his chair around, he gazed out the window. He could see the entire city of Roald spread out before him and the sight filled him with pleasure. With the ownership of the uranium deposit and full control of the colony, mastery of the entire satellite and possibly the star system itself was only one short step away.

The door opened and Ed Bush hurried breathlessly into the room. "You sent for me, boss?" he asked.

Vidac swung around to face his lieutenant. "How much do you know about electronics and astrophysics?" he snapped.

"Why, as much as the average guy, I guess," answered Bush.

"Well, you're going to learn more," said Vidac. He began to outline his plan quickly. "I want you to hang around Sykes and the cadets on this new education project. They're going to make study spools for the colony kids. Manning will be in charge of electronics and astrophysics. Now here's what I want you to do . . ."

While the lieutenant governor was outlining his plan to his henchman, the three cadets were entering their new quarters on the lower floor of the Administration Building.

"Can you imagine that guy?" asked Astro. "Picking on Roger in front of Professor Sykes? He as good as told the professor to give Roger a hard time!"

As the big Venusian slammed one hamlike fist into the other, Tom nudged him in the ribs and then turned to Roger with a smile.

"Don't worry about it, Roger," said Tom. "We've got a job to do. Getting the school system going here on Roald is important, and whether you like him or not, Professor Sykes is the best man to handle it."

"I realize that, Tom," said Roger. "But I don't know how long I can—"

Jeff Marshall suddenly appeared in the doorway of their quarters. "Professor Sykes wants to see us right away, fellows," he announced. "And watch your temper, Roger. Just do the best you can, and the professor will leave you alone."

"You said it," agreed Tom. "Nothing in the universe talks as loudly as hard work. Let's all show him."

The three cadets followed the enlisted spaceman out of the room and headed toward Sykes's quarters. Tom's thoughts were confused. He wasn't sure of his feelings any more. So much had happened since their departure from Space Academy. Then, suddenly, he realized that he hadn't sent his second report to Captain Strong. He wasn't even sure whether his first report had gotten through. He turned to Astro and remarked casually, "I wonder what Captain Strong is doing right now?"

"I don't know," replied Astro. "But I sure wish he was here!"

"Say it again, spaceboy," growled Roger. "Say it again!"

At that moment over fifty-five billion miles away, in his office high in the Tower of Galileo, Commander Walters was talking with Captain Steve Strong and Dr. Joan Dale. The stern-faced, gray-haired commander of Space Academy frowned as he read a report Joan Dale had just given him.

"Are you sure of this, Joan?" he asked.

"I'm positive, Commander," replied the beautiful young doctor of astrophysics. "The tests are conclusive. There is uranium on Roald!"

"But I don't understand why it wasn't discovered before this?" mused Strong. "It's been nearly a year since the first exploratory expedition out to Roald."

"Samplings of the soil of Roald were taken from all sections of the satellite, Steve," replied Joan. "On-the-spot tests were made by the scientists of course, but there were no indications of uranium then. But cadets majoring in planetary geology tested the soil samples as part of their training. Several of them reported uranium findings. And I checked all their examinations carefully, besides making further tests of my own. That report is the result." She indicated the paper on Walters' desk.

"But you say the deposit is probably a large one," Walters protested. "How could it have been missed?"

"Not necessarily large, sir," said Joan, "but certainly of the purest quality."

Walters looked up at Strong. "Well, Steve?"

"Joan told me about it, sir," said Strong. "And since an investigation is probably the next step, I came over, hoping you'd let me go along." He paused and looked at Joan.

"Steve would also like to see his crew of Space Cadets." Joan smiled. "He hasn't received a report from them yet, and I think he's worried they might be involved in some mischief!"

"No report, eh?" asked Walters.

"No, sir," replied Steve. "I thought one would be waiting for me when I got back from Pluto. But there wasn't any."

"Ummmh!" mused Walters. He looked at his calendar. "About time for them to send in a second report too. Tell you what, Steve. They might be having a tough time setting up things out there on Roald. Suppose you get things organized to investigate the uranium report. And if no word comes in from the cadets by the end of the week, then you can blast off."

"Thank you, sir," said Strong. "Will you excuse me, sir? I'd like to get to work right away."

At Walters' nod, Strong saluted briskly and left the office. Walters turned to Joan.

"You know, I don't think he's half as interested in finding a big uranium deposit as he is in seeing those boys!"

* * * * *

In four separate soundproof cubicles in a small office in the Administration Building on Roald, the three space cadets and Jeff Marshall racked their brains to remember simple equations and formulas, knowledge learned years ago but long-since forgotten, for the more complicated subjects of space, time, and rocket travel. Now, trying to recall simple arithmetic and other elementary studies, the cadets and Marshall worked eighteen hours a day. Speaking directly into soundscribers and filling what seemed to be miles of audio tape, the four spacemen attempted to build a comprehensive library of a hundred carefully selected subjects for the children of Roald. Professor Sykes listened to the study spools as they were completed. He listened carefully, reviewed their work, edited it, and made notes for follow-up comment. Then, at the end of the day, he would hold a final meeting with them, outline what he wanted the next day, and reject spools that he felt were not satisfactory. For older children's studies, the three cadets and Jeff had divided their work into four classifications. Roger covered electronics, astrophysics, astrogation, and allied fields. Astro took charge of rockets, missiles, power machinery, and applied uses of atomic energy. Jeff's work was biological, bacteriological, mineralogical, and geological. Tom covered social studies, government, economy, and history.

Resting as comfortably as possible, each of the four spacemen would sit and think. And when he had gone as far back as he could in his memory of formal education and acquired knowledge, he would begin to talk into the soundscriber. Of all the spools, Tom's were edited the least. And Professor Sykes had unbent enough to compliment the curly-haired cadet for his lucid thinking and acute memory. Astro's work needed the most editing. The giant Venusian found it difficult to explain what he did when he repaired atomic power plants, or how he could look at a piece of machinery and know instinctively when it was out of order. He worked twice as hard as the others, simply because Sykes made him do everything over.

On the other hand, Roger sailed along as smoothly as a jet boat. His grasp of the fundamentals in his field made it easy for him to fill the study spools with important information. Jeff, too, found it easy to explain the growth of plants, the function of bacteria, the formation of planet crusts, and other allied subjects.

So, day after day, Tom, Astro, Roger, and Jeff Marshall spent their waking hours in the cubicles searching their minds for every last precious drop of knowledge they could impart to the children of Roald.

Vidac's warning to Professor Sykes to keep an eye on Roger had been forgotten by everyone in the concerted effort to do a good job. And when the cadets and Jeff left their work one night after a loud argument between the professor and Roger over the best way to explain the theory of captive planets, they thought nothing of it. The argument hadn't been unusual. It had happened many times on the same score. Professor Sykes was prone to favor dry, factual explanations. And the cadets believed some of the theories needed explanations in terms a youngster could understand. Sykes did not object to this method, but was wary of losing facts and clarity in the method of instruction. In this particular case, Roger had given in to Sykes, but only after a heated argument. And when they went back to their quarters, there was none of the usual discussion. They were too tired. They fell asleep as soon as their heads touched their pillows.

The next morning, still groggy, their heads filled with facts and figures, buzzing with dates and explanations, they returned to their cubicles for more of the same. Sykes met them at the office door.

"Well, Manning!" he snapped. "You still insist you know more, *and* can teach better than I, eh?" He glowered at the cadet.

"I don't understand, sir," said Roger.

"You don't, eh?" screamed Sykes. "You came back here last night and changed that spool to *your* liking!"

"I did what?" asked Roger, incredulous. Only a few moments before he could hardly drag himself from his bunk. The idea of returning to the office before the required time was incredible. "I'm sorry, sir," he said, "but I only got out of bed a few minutes ago."

Ed Bush and several colonists suddenly appeared and Sykes whirled around to face them.

"Well! What do you want?" he demanded.

"Governor Vidac said we could pick up some of the spools that were ready," said Bush.

"Well, there isn't anything ready now," growled Sykes. "When I'm finished, I'll let Vidac know." He turned back to Roger.

"Well, Manning? What have you got to say for yourself?"

"I don't know what you're talking about, sir!" answered Roger.

"Cadet Manning," shouted Sykes, "do you remember our conversation last night on the subject of circular motion of captive planets around a sun star?"

"Yes, sir," said Roger.

"And do you recall your childish manner of explaining it?" sneered Sykes.

"Now just a minute, sir," said Roger, "I might be wrong— but—"

"Quiet!" The professor was screaming now. He turned around and inserted a study spool in a soundscriber. Turning it on he waited, glaring at Roger. The blond-haired cadet's voice came over the machine's loud-speaker clearly and precisely.

" . . . the idea of motion of one satellite around a mother planet, or planet around a sun star, can best be explained by the use of a rock tied to the end of a rope. If you swing the rope around your head, the rock will maintain a steady position, following a measured orbit. The planets, and their captive satellites, work on the same principle, with the gravity of the mother planet substituted for the rope, and the satellite for the rock . . ."

Sykes stopped the machine, turned, and glared at Roger. "Do you deny that that is your voice?"

Roger shook his head. "It's my voice all right but—"

"*And* do you deny that last night, before we left, it was decided that my explanation would be used?"

Roger's face reddened. "No, sir," he said tightly.

"Then how do you explain that *your* voice with *your* explanation is now on the master spool?" screamed Sykes.

"I—I—can't explain it, sir," said Roger, fighting to control his temper.

"I can!" snapped Sykes. "You sneaked back in here last night and substituted your original recording—the one I threw out!"

"But he couldn't have done that, Professor," interjected Tom. "He was asleep all night!"

"Were you awake all night, Corbett?" asked Sykes coldly.

"No, sir," replied Tom.

"Then you couldn't possibly know if he was sleeping or down here recording, could you?"

"No, sir," said Tom quietly.

"Cadet Manning, this is the most disgusting, disgraceful performance I've ever seen by a Space Cadet!"

"Then you're calling me a liar, sir," said Roger quietly, "when I deny that I did it."

"Can you explain it?" demanded Sykes.

Roger shook his head and remained silent.

"Get out!" screamed Sykes. "Vidac warned me about you! Go on! Get out! I won't work with a liar and a cheat!"

Before anyone could stop him, Roger leaped forward and stood in front of Sykes, grabbing him by the front of his uniform. "I've had enough of your insults and accusations!" he shouted. "If you weren't an old man, I'd drag you out of that Solar Guard uniform and beat your ears off! You're so crazy, you make everyone around you nuts! If you have any complaints about my work, put them in writing and give them to the governor!"

He turned and stalked out of the office.

"Roger, wait!" called Tom, rushing after his unit mate with Astro at his heels.

The colonists began to whisper to each other excitedly, but Ed Bush merely stood in the doorway and smiled!

CHAPTER 14

"That's right," sneered Winters. "Professor Sykes has disappeared and Vidac wants to talk to you!"

The burly spaceman stood in the open door of the cadets' quarters, legs spread apart, hands on the paralo-ray guns strapped to his side. Tom, Roger, and Astro eyed the man sleepily.

"Say that again," said Tom.

"I said Vidac wants to talk to you!" Winters shouted. "Now pile out of those bunks before I pull you out!"

Astro sat up and looked at Winters. His voice rumbled menacingly. "I'll give you five seconds to get out of here," he said quietly. "And if you don't, I'll ram those ray guns down your throat! One—two—three—"

Winters tried to match Astro's withering gaze and finally backed out the doorway. "Vidac wants to see you on the double, and that means, *double!*" He disappeared from view.

Tom and Roger were already out of their bunks and pulling on their uniforms.

"What do you think?" asked Roger, looking at Tom.

"I don't know, Roger," said Tom, "but I don't like the looks of it."

Astro jumped lightly to the floor. "I kinda wish Winters had tried something," he said with a smile. "I need a little early-morning exercise."

"Good thing he didn't," commented Roger dryly. "We're in enough trouble without you mauling one of Vidac's pet boys."

Tom listened halfheartedly to the chatter of his unit mates. He was thinking ahead to their meeting with Vidac. Since Roger's argument with the professor, they had continued their work, but under a severe strain. They had finally finished the series of study spools the night before, and Tom felt sure that Vidac had waited until the work was finished before he called them on the carpet. And then, too, there was the disappearance of Professor Sykes that Winters had mentioned. The young cadet felt there was trouble ahead.

A few moments later the three cadets presented themselves to Vidac in his office in the Administration Building.

The lieutenant governor was seated behind his desk and appeared to be very tired. Tom saluted smartly and stepped forward.

"Polaris unit reporting, sir," said Tom.

"Where is Professor Sykes?" demanded Vidac abruptly without even acknowledging the salute.

"Why, I—I don't know, sir," replied Tom.

"How about you, Manning? Astro?" asked Vidac, turning to the other cadets. "You have anything to say?"

"We only heard about it ten minutes ago, sir," volunteered Roger.

"I'll bet!" snapped Vidac. He got up and stepped around his desk to face the cadets. "You three were the last ones to be seen with the professor. What happened last night?"

"We finished the study spools and left him in the office, sir," said Tom. "Then we went for a swim in the pool and had a bite to eat before hitting the sack. That's all."

"Did anyone see you in the pool?" asked Vidac.

"I doubt it, sir. We didn't notice anyone around," said Astro. "It was pretty late."

"Did anyone see you at the mess hall when you went to get a bite?" pursued Vidac. "Surely there must be someone who can substantiate your story."

The three cadets looked at each other. "I guess not, sir," said Roger. "It was pretty late. After midnight."

Vidac eyed them curiously. "And you're sure you saw no one, and that no one saw you?"

"We can't be sure that no one saw us, sir," said Tom, "but I doubt it. As Roger said, it was after midnight."

Vidac whirled and sat down again. He pressed a small button on his desk and waited, silently considering the cadets, his eyes cool and level. The door opened and Governor Hardy walked in, followed by several men.

Tom suddenly realized that it was the first time they had seen the governor in nearly six weeks.

"Have you found Professor Sykes?" he demanded.

Vidac shook his head, then turned to the other men. Tom, with a sudden sinking feeling in the pit of his stomach, recognized them as the colonists who had been with Ed Bush when Roger had his last argument with the professor.

"Did you hear Cadet Manning threaten Professor Sykes?" asked Vidac.

"Yes, sir," replied one of the colonists.

"What did he say?" asked Vidac. "Repeat it for Governor Hardy."

The colonist quoted Roger's threat almost word for word and Tom noted grimly that the witness made the most of the fact that he and Astro had followed Roger out of the office after the argument. The implication was clear that they were part of the threat.

Vidac then turned to Ed Bush. "Bush, did you see the cadets last night?"

"Yes, sir," said Bush.

"Where?" demanded Vidac.

"Leaving the swimming pool with the professor."

"With the pro—!" exclaimed Tom.

"Shut up, Corbett!" barked Vidac, and then turned to Astro. "Did you say you went swimming *alone?*"

"We did!" exclaimed the Venusian. "We left the professor at the office. We did not see him again after that. He did not go swimming with us."

Vidac turned to Winters. "Did you see the cadets last night, Winters?"

"Yes, sir," replied the spaceman. "I had the graveyard watch and I was in the galley having a cup of coffee. I saw the cadets enter the galley just as I was leaving."

"Were they alone?" asked Vidac.

"No, sir," said Winters. "Professor Sykes was with them."

"That's a lie!" shouted Roger. "We were alone!"

Vidac merely looked at Roger and then turned back to Winters. "Then what happened?"

"Well," said Winters, "they got into an argument, the cadets and Sykes. It was about the movement of a captive planet, or something like that. Anyway, there was a scuffle, and all of a sudden the big cadet"—he indicated Astro—"picked up the professor and carried him out of the galley. The other two followed."

"Didn't the professor put up a fight?" asked Vidac.

"Oh, yes, sir," said Winters. "But he didn't have a chance against the three cadets."

"Why didn't you do something about it?" Governor Hardy suddenly broke in.

"I tried, sir," replied Winters calmly. "I ran after them, but they all piled into a converted jet boat and blasted out of there."

"Then what did you do?" asked Vidac.

"That's when I came to get you, sir," said Winters. "And we started looking for them." Winters paused. "Ah—pardon me, sir, but can I go now? I've been up all night and I'm pretty tired."

Vidac nodded and Winters left the room.

"You mean you've been up all night looking for the cadets?" asked Hardy. "Weren't they in their quarters?"

"No, sir," replied Vidac and turned to the cadets. "Well," he demanded, "what have you got to say for yourselves?"

The three cadets were silent.

"I must warn you," continued Vidac, "this is a serious matter and anything you say may be used against you. But on the other hand, if you speak freely and are willing to co-operate, I will do what I can to lessen your punishment."

Hardy suddenly stepped forward and slammed his fist on Vidac's desk. "None of that! There'll be no favors to criminals!" He turned to the cadets angrily.

"What did you do with the professor?" he demanded.

The cadets kept silent.

"Where did you take him?" he shouted.

Neither Tom, Roger, or Astro batted an eyelash. They kept their eyes front and their lips tight.

"I warn you, you'll spend the rest of your lives on a prison rock if you don't answer!"

Tom finally turned and looked straight at the governor. "May I speak, sir?"

"Only if you tell me what you did with Professor Sykes," replied Hardy angrily.

"You have not asked us, sir," said Tom coolly, "to tell our side of the story. You are accusing us of a crime and have already assumed that we are guilty. We are not."

Bush pulled a paralo-ray gun from his belt and said, "All right, march!"

"Do you deny it?" asked Hardy.

"We deny everything," said Tom flatly.

Hardy whirled around to face the colonists, Vidac, and Bush. "I want it clearly understood by everyone here that Space Cadets Tom Corbett, Roger Manning, and Astro, in the face of testimony given by eyewitnesses as to their argument with Professor Sykes, and their later abduction of the professor, do now conspire to withhold information which might help save the professor's life!" He turned to Vidac. "I want them arrested and held for investigation of their activities last night. Confine them to their quarters."

Vidac stood up and nodded his head to Bush. "Take them away. Keep a guard outside their quarters at all times."

"Yes, sir," said Bush. He pulled a paralo-ray gun from his belt and cocked it. "All right, march!"

The cadets of the *Polaris* unit spun on their heels in unison and marched from the room in perfect order.

* * * * *

"Attention! Attention! This is Captain Strong in rocket cruiser *Orion* calling central communications control, Roald! Come in, Roald! *Orion* to Roald! Come in!"

Aboard the space cruiser, Captain Steve Strong tried again and again to contact the star colony. For nearly five days, blasting through space at emergency speed, the Solar Guard captain had tried to contact the satellite, but to no avail. He snapped off the audioceiver and slumped back in his chair, a worried frown on his face.

When the second report from the *Polaris* unit had failed to come in, Strong had received permission from Commander Walters to blast off immediately for Roald. Walters agreed that it would be better for the captain to go alone, since the uranium discovery must be kept an absolute secret. Working by remote control relays from the control deck, Captain Strong handled the ship as easily as a jet boat and he kept the atomic reactors wide open.

He stared into the astrogation prism and sighted on the cold light of the sun star Wolf 359. Still unable to see the satellite circling the star, the captain's thoughts were on the past rather than the future. He still couldn't find any reasonable explanation for his suddenly having been taken off the Roald colony project and sent on the minor mission to Pluto. He had often thought about the man who had replaced him, Paul Vidac. Strong had heard the name before and associated it with something unpleasant. He couldn't put his finger on what it was, since he had never met the man. Certainly there was nothing illegal about him. His record had been carefully checked, or he would never have been put in the position of trust he held now. Still there was a persistent notion in Strong's head that something was wrong.

The young captain turned and walked the deck of the huge empty ship, still deep in thought. He considered the fact that no reports had come through to the Academy from the colony at all. Not merely from the Space Cadets, but from the expedition itself. Only the sketchiest details had been audioed back during the trip and absolutely nothing since their scheduled arrival on the satellite. A sudden cold wave of fear gripped the space officer. He wondered if they had arrived safely!

He shook off the horrible thought. There must be a simple, logical explanation for it all. Establishing a star colony was no easy matter. Communications could be easily disrupted for any number of reasons.

Strong forced himself to forget it. It was still a long way to the satellite and there was no point in worrying about a fact until it was established to be a fact. He stretched out on a bunk and moments later was asleep, while the giant ship hurtled through the dark void toward its destination with a thousand electronic hands and eyes to guide it safely across the immense gulf of space.

CHAPTER 15

"Is he still out there?" Tom whispered.

"Yeah," growled Astro. "He hasn't moved."

"They're not taking any chances," said Roger. "When they change the guard, they take out their ray guns, just in case."

The three cadets were crowded around the door of their quarters with Astro down on his hands and knees, trying to see through a small crack. The big cadet straightened up and shook his head.

"I guess it's useless," he sighed. "Vidac is making sure we stay here."

"Well," said Roger disgustedly, "if we don't get out pretty soon, we won't—" He didn't finish the sentence. At that moment the door suddenly opened and Bush stepped in, two paralo-ray guns in his hands, cocked and ready to fire. Behind him was Hyram Logan and his daughter, Jane.

"You got ten minutes," said Bush, "and one funny move out of any of you and I'll blast you silly."

He closed the door and the click of the lock could be heard ominously.

"Mr. Logan!" exclaimed Tom. "How'd you manage to get in here?"

"Sonny," replied the Venusian farmer, "when you're dealing with crooks, you have to act like a crook!" He smiled and added, "I bought my way in here!"

"You mean that Vidac doesn't know you're here?" asked Astro.

"No," said Jane. "But we had to come. Vidac was going to—" She stopped and turned to her father. "Maybe you'd better tell them, Father."

"Well," said Logan slowly, "we just heard that Vidac is going to hold trial for you three boys right here on Roald."

"Trial!" exclaimed Astro.

"How'd you find that out?" asked Tom.

"They called all the colonists together and gave us pieces of paper with numbers on them," said Logan. "Then they put all the numbers into a bowl and picked twelve of them out again. The people that held those numbers were told that they were going to be the jury at your trial for the murder of Professor Sykes!"

"Murder?" exclaimed Roger.

"Blast my jets!" roared Astro. "They can't do that! We're under Solar Guard jurisdiction!"

"That's what I told them," snorted Logan. "You see, my number was pulled. I got up and opened my big mouth. I should have kept quiet and sat on the jury, and then had my say where it would have meant something!"

"Then they took you off the jury?" asked Roger.

"Yep," said Logan. "Me and everyone else they thought might be prejudiced!"

"We came to tell you," said Jane, "because we wanted you to know what was going on and to see if there was anything we could do to help."

"We already tried to help in a lot of ways," said Logan. "We tried to get that space jerk outside to let you escape. I offered him—well, I offered him a lot, but he wouldn't do it."

"What are you going to do?" asked Jane, looking at Tom.

"I don't know, Jane," said Tom. "But we've certainly got to do something. If we ever stand trial here on Roald—"

Tom was interrupted by a loud banging on the door, followed by the click of the lock. Then the door was opened and Bush stepped inside.

"All right, Logan," said Bush. "Time's up!"

"But—but," complained Logan, "we've only been here two minutes!"

"Time's up, I said," sneered Bush. He raised his ray guns threateningly.

"Well, I guess we'd better go," said Logan. He turned and shook hands with each of the cadets. "Good luck, boys," he said with a smile. "Don't worry. We'll find someway of getting you out of this mess!"

"Thanks for telling us, sir," said Tom.

"Telling you what?" demanded Bush.

"That the world is round and that you're a square-headed space crawler," said Roger casually.

"A real big mouth, eh!" snarled Bush. "Why, I oughta—" He raised his guns again, but just at the moment Jane walked into the line of fire and stood there quietly. Bush stepped back. It was just enough to break the tension.

"Go on!" Bush growled. "Get out of here!"

"Don't get rough," said Logan, "or I might tell your boss you took a bribe to let us see the cadets!" With a parting wink at the boys, he followed Jane out.

Just as Bush started to close the door, Tom stepped forward. "How about something to eat," he demanded, "and some story tapes to pass away the time?"

"Yeah," said Roger, picking up Tom's cue, "and we don't want anything you'd select either. It might be too infantile! Send Jeff Marshall up here so we can get what we want!"

"I'll see about it," sneered Bush, slamming the door behind him.

"Are you thinking what I'm thinking?" Roger asked Tom.

"Yes. If there is anyone we can trust, it's Jeff. Let's hope that space jerk outside comes through!"

"Well," growled Astro, "if worse comes to worse, we can always jump him."

"Uh—uh," said Tom, shaking his head. "We wouldn't get past the first corridor. If we escape, and we will, we've got to have help from someone on the outside!"

"But won't they be watching Jeff too?" asked Astro.

"Sure they will, but we've got to take that chance. If Vidac holds us for trial here on Roald, and we're convicted, the only place for a review of the case will be the Solar Council Chamber back on Earth."

"Well, what's wrong with that?" asked Astro.

"I'll tell you what's wrong with it," said Roger. "Before the case would come up for a review, we would have already spent at least two years on a prison rock!"

Meanwhile, in his office in the Administration Building, Lieutenant Governor Vidac listened with mounting apprehension to a report from the communications control officer of Roald.

"We just received a message from Captain Strong aboard the Solar Guard cruiser *Orion* requesting landing data here on Roald," the voice crackled impersonally over the televeiver.

"How far out is he?" asked Vidac, suddenly growing pale.

"He should arrive within four hours."

"All right," said Vidac, regaining his composure. "Give him all the information he needs."

"What about the instrument disturbance?"

"Tell him everything."

"Yes, sir," replied the control officer, and the televeiver screen went blank.

Vidac got up and began to pace the floor, pondering the reasons for Strong's sudden unannounced visit. He could be coming to check on the Space Cadets, he thought. Or it might be a routine check of the progress of the colony. Or he might know about the uranium. There had been an investigation of the soil on the satellite by the original expedition. But if they had known anything about it, reasoned Vidac, it would have been claimed for the Solar Alliance.

No, Vidac shook his head. He's not here to investigate the uranium, he's here either to check on the cadets or make a routine inspection of the colony. And if it's the former, he'd give Strong enough proof to bury the cadets on a prison rock for life.

Vidac turned to the televeiver. "Get the spaceport," he ordered. "Tell the spaceport officer to prepare a welcoming party to blast off in ten minutes. They will meet Captain Strong of the Solar Guard in the cruiser *Orion*. Communications control will give them his position." He flipped off the televeiver and settled back in his chair, smiling. Nothing in the world like a big fuss to throw a man off guard, he thought. And Steve Strong, as the first visitor from Earth since the colony was founded, would get a tremendous welcome!

* * * * *

" . . . Are you sure?" asked Tom, his face brightening. "You heard it yourself?"

Jeff Marshall smiled. "Roald is going crazy. They're preparing the biggest welcome for a spaceman since Jon Builker's return from his first trip in space!"

"Boy," said Astro, "what a break!" He slapped Roger on the back. "We'll be out of this can an hour after Captain Strong lands!"

"I knew you wanted me to help you try to escape," said Jeff. "I had already begun to make plans."

"No need for that now," said Tom. "If we tried to escape, we'd be doing the very thing Vidac would want us to do. He could say it was an admission of guilt."

Roger agreed with a nod of his head. "There's only one thing that bothers me now."

"What's that?" asked Astro.

"Professor Sykes," he said. "We've been so worried about our own necks, we've forgotten about him."

"Well," said Astro, "what about him?"

"What really happened to him," mused Roger, "and why?"

"I wish I knew," said Tom. "But I'll bet Vidac knows."

"Sure," agreed Roger. "But I still say why and what?"

The blond-haired cadet looked around at the faces of his friends. There was no reply to his question.

* * * * *

Every citizen of Roald, man, woman, and child, was at the spaceport to watch the giant cruiser *Orion* settle slowly to the ground. Vidac watched it through squinting eyes. He had secretly hoped that the uranium disturbances would cause the ship to crash, thus eliminating his difficulties before they could begin, but he couldn't help admiring the way the big cruiser was handled. When the hatch opened and Captain Strong stepped out, resplendent in his black-and-gold uniform, there was a spontaneous roar of welcome from the ground. Vidac stepped forward immediately to greet the Solar Guard officer.

"I'm Paul Vidac, Captain Strong. Lieutenant governor of Roald. Governor Hardy is very busy and asked me to welcome you and to convey his apologies for not greeting you personally."

"Thank you," said Strong and shook hands with Vidac. He turned around and looked over the crowd. "But I seem to be missing several other welcomers."

"Ah, I presume you mean the Space Cadets," stammered Vidac.

Strong looked at the lieutenant governor. "Yes, I mean the Space Cadets. Where are they?"

Vidac tried to meet Strong's level gaze, but his eyes fell away. "They are under arrest!" he said finally.

"Arrest!" cried Strong. "For what?"

"The murder of Professor Sykes."

"Murder? Professor Sykes?" asked Strong. "Explain yourself!"

"This is hardly the place to discuss it. Shall we go to my office?" asked Vidac.

"Where is the professor's body?" asked Strong.

"It hasn't been found yet," replied Vidac uneasily.

"Then how can the cadets be charged with murder if you can't produce a body?" demanded Strong.

Vidac paused a moment. He was thrown off guard by Strong's shrewd observation. "They are also being held for abduction of the professor," said Vidac. "We have eyewitnesses."

"Take me to them," said Strong.

"I'm afraid that will be impossible at the moment," said Vidac. "The colonists are expecting a little show for their enthusiastic welcome."

"Take me to the cadets," Strong demanded. "And that means immediately!"

Vidac wavered under the Solar Guard captain's withering gaze. He nodded and turned away.

As Strong pushed through the crowd of welcoming colonists, someone tugged at his sleeve and whispered into his ear.

"Don't believe all you hear!" Strong turned to see the face of Hyram Logan. Before he could reply, Logan disappeared into the crowd.

"Well, Captain Strong? Are you coming?" asked Vidac.

Strong turned and followed him through the crowd. He could feel danger on this satellite. He could feel it and he could read it in the faces of the people around him.

CHAPTER 16

"I'll leave you here," said Vidac to Captain Strong as the two spacemen stood in front of the Administration Building. "Take the slidestairs up to the seventh floor. First corridor to the left. There will be a guard outside their door. Give him this note and there won't be any trouble."

Strong looked at the lieutenant governor coolly. "There better not be," he said.

"That's a strange attitude to take, Captain," said Vidac.

"Vidac," said Strong coldly, "I want you to know right now that I don't like this setup. There are many things cadets might be, but they are not kidnappers or murderers!"

"I intend to prove otherwise!" asserted Vidac.

"I figured you would," said Strong, "but you still have to produce Professor Sykes's body."

"Don't worry, Captain." Vidac smiled. "My men are searching for it now. We'll find it."

"When you do, Vidac," said Strong grimly, "and he happens to be alive, make sure he stays that way, eh?" The Solar Guard captain wheeled and entered the Administration Building before Vidac could answer.

Inside, he found the slidestairs and rode up to the seventh level. Taking the first corridor to the left, he rounded a corner to find Ed Bush standing in front of the door to the cadets' quarters. As he approached, Bush took out his paralo-ray gun and held it on Strong.

"That's far enough, mister," said Bush.

"Do you realize what you're doing?" demanded Strong.

"Never mind what I'm doing," snapped Bush. "Who are you and what do you want?"

"You'd better get spacewise, mister! It's against the law to hold a weapon on an officer of the Solar Guard! I'm Captain Strong and I want to see the cadets!"

"No one gets inside without a pass from Governor Vidac," Bush answered surlily.

Strong pulled out the note and handed it over brusquely. Bush glanced at it and handed it back.

"O.K.," he said. "You got ten minutes." He unlocked the door and stepped aside.

Strong was furious at this treatment. But he held his temper in check, realizing he had to talk to the cadets first and find out what had happened. He would deal with Bush later. He stepped past Bush and opened the door.

"*Polaris* unit—stand to!" he yelled.

Seated around the table, the three cadets stared at their captain in disbelief, then instinctively rose and snapped to attention. Their backs were straight and their eyes forward, but it was impossible for them to keep smiles off their faces. Suppressing his own elation, Strong managed to stride in front of them in mock inspection, but then could no longer hold back an answering smile.

"Unit—stand easy!"

Like three happy puppies the cadets swarmed over their skipper, pounding him on the back, grabbing his hands, and mauling him until he had to cry out for peace.

"Take it easy," he cried. "Relax, will you! You'll tear me apart!"

"You're the happiest sight I've seen in weeks, sir!" shouted Tom.

"Yeah," drawled Roger, grinning from ear to ear. "I couldn't be happier if you had brought along a ship full of space dolls!"

"When did you get here, sir?" asked Astro. "Why didn't you let us know?"

The questions tumbled out of the boys' mouths thick and fast, and Strong let them chatter until their initial burst of elation had worn itself out. Then, after quickly bringing them up to date on all news of the Academy, and news of Earth, he pulled up a chair and faced them solemnly. The three cadets braced themselves to tell him about their experiences since leaving Atom City.

"There's a lot to tell, sir," began Tom. "But we're only going to give you the facts as we know them, sir. And then let you decide."

Then starting from the beginning, when they were first relieved of their stations on the *Polaris* on the way out to the satellite, the three cadets related their experiences with Vidac, Hardy, and Professor Sykes. They ended with a detailed account of their being held for the disappearance of the professor.

"And you say that the colonists were forced to pay for their food on the trip out?" asked Strong incredulously.

"Yes, sir," said Tom. "And later, after the ships crashed, there was a shortage of farm tools and equipment, which meant that the colonists would have to farm with chemicals. Vidac made them sign over part of their future profits and mortgage their land holdings to get the chemicals."

"And four hundred ships crashed in landing? Hasn't anybody figured out why yet?" Strong asked.

Roger shook his head. "The instruments just went out, sir," he said. "I never saw anything like it, and when the professor wanted to go down in a jet boat first to investigate, Vidac insisted on taking the *Polaris* down, anyway. He brought her in by the seat of his pants . . ."

"Only because Tom took over when he got cold feet," chimed in Astro.

"Yeah," agreed Roger. "But the others couldn't do it. They just splashed in."

"And there hasn't been any explanation of why the instruments went out?"

"I haven't heard any, sir," said Astro. "Professor Sykes started out right after we landed to investigate the satellite, but I never heard anything more about it. When I asked him one day if he had found anything, he told me to mind my own business."

"And now you're accused of abducting and murdering the professor," mused Strong.

"That's it, sir," said Tom. "As I said, we didn't want to give you anything but the facts as we know them. There are a lot of incidents that would show Vidac is trying to pull something funny, but nothing that could be proved."

Strong nodded. "Well, it certainly looks as though Vidac is—"

Strong was suddenly interrupted by Bush who stepped into the room arrogantly, paralo-ray gun in hand.

"Time's up!" he yelled, waving the gun at Strong.

"I've warned you about holding a weapon on a Solar Guard officer," snapped Strong, rising to face the man. "Either put that thing away or use it."

"Hasn't anybody figured out why four hundred ships crashed in landing?" Strong asked.

Bush glanced at the smiling cadets and turned back to Strong.

"Your time is up," he growled. "Get out!"

"I said," replied Strong coldly, "either use that thing or put it away!"

Bush glared at Strong, but the gun in his hand began to waver. "I said your time's up!" he repeated, but there was considerably less conviction in his voice.

Suddenly Strong stepped forward and grabbed the man's wrist, forcing the gun down. As Bush started to struggle, Strong tightened his grip, and the victim's face grew white with pain. Slowly Bush's fingers opened and the paralo-ray weapon dropped to the floor.

"Now pick it up and get out of here!" barked Strong, releasing Bush's arm. "I'm going to stay with the cadets as long as I want. And if you ever pull a gun on me again, I'll make you eat it!"

He turned his back to Bush and faced the cadets again. Bush dove for the gun, raised it threateningly, then suddenly walked out of the room, slamming the door as hard as he could. The cadets sighed in relief and Strong smiled.

"Let's see what Vidac makes of that," he said. "Now, let's get down to business. There's only one thing I can do right now."

"Yes, sir?" asked Tom, waiting attentively.

"I'm going to talk with a few of the colonists and see what else I can pick up. Meantime, you just take it easy. And if that space jerk outside gives you any trouble"—Strong paused and smiled—"show him a few of your wrestling tricks, Astro."

The big Venusian nodded enthusiastically. "My pleasure, Captain."

Strong stood up and shook hands with each of them. "From what you've told me," he said, "I think I should see Hyram Logan first."

"Yes, sir," said Tom. "He's sort of the spokesman for the rest of the colonists. He can give you a lot of information."

"Good!" said Strong. "Where will I find him?"

Tom gave directions and the captain left the three cadets with a smile. "Don't worry. We'll see this through. In a short while you'll be on duty again."

A half-hour later, in one of the converted jet boats, Steve Strong sped along the smooth broad streets and flat level highways of the colony. He was heading for the Logan farm and the long drive through the Roald countryside would ordinarily have been interesting and enjoyable. But the Solar Guard captain was preoccupied with his own thoughts. A name kept repeating itself over and over in his mind. Hardy—Hardy—Hardy. Why hadn't the governor done something about Vidac? Where was he when the colonists were forced to pay for their food? Why hadn't he checked on the cadets' statement that their report hadn't been sent out? Strong made a mental note to check the logbook of the *Polaris* when he returned.

Suddenly, ahead of him, he saw a young boy walking along the highway. He slowed down and stopped beside him.

"Hello, Sonny," called Strong with a smile. "Can you tell me where I can find the Logan farm?"

The boy stared at Strong, eyes wide. "Sure thing, Mister, er—I mean—Captain. I'm Billy Logan."

"Well, hop in, Billy!" said Strong. "I'll give you a lift!"

"Thanks," replied the boy and jumped in beside Strong. "It's about a mile up the road, then we turn off." He couldn't keep his eyes off Strong's black-and-gold uniform. "I'm going to be a Space Cadet when I get old enough," he gulped breathlessly.

"You are?" asked Strong. "That's fine. You have to study very hard."

"I know," said Billy, "I'm starting already! Tom, Roger, and Astro lent me books and study spools to work on. Why, I bet I know every single Academy regulation right now!"

Strong laughed. "I wouldn't be surprised!"

"We turn off here," said Billy, indicating a narrow road branching off the main highway. "We live about three miles down. Out in the wilderness. By the stars, it's so lonely out here sometimes, I wish I was back on Venus!"

"If you want to be a spaceman," said Strong, "you have to learn not to be lonely. Why, I just made a trip out from Atom City all by myself. Didn't bother me a bit!"

"You did?" cried Billy. "Gosh!"

He was so awed by Strong's solo trip out to the satellite that he remained silent the rest of the trip.

A few moments later Strong pulled up at a small crystal structure, just off the road. He had no sooner stopped, than Billy was out of the car yelling to his father and sister at the top of his voice that they had a visitor.

Hyram Logan came from around the back of the house to greet Strong, and Jane, who had been busy in the kitchen preparing supper, came to meet the young officer, wiping her hands on her apron.

"Mighty glad to see the Solar Guard remembered we're out here," said Logan as he led Strong into the house. Seated comfortably in the living room, Strong brought up the purpose of his visit right away.

"I've just finished talking to the cadets, Mr. Logan, and they've been telling me some strange stories about Vidac and Governor Hardy. I'd like to hear what you have to say about it."

"I can say everything in one sentence, Captain," snorted Logan. "Those space crawlers are trying to take everything we have away from us!"

And for three hours Strong listened as the Venusian farmer talked. When the farmer had finished, Strong asked only one question.

"Why didn't Governor Hardy do something?"

"I can't explain that," said Logan. "When we were forced to pay for our food on the way out, we signed a petition and sent it to the governor. But we never heard anything about it. Of course Vidac could have intercepted it."

"Well, thank you, Mr. Logan," said Strong, getting up.

"Won't you stay for supper, Captain?" asked Jane.

"Yeah, please stay, sir," pleaded Billy. "I'd like to hear about your trip out here all by yourself."

Strong laughed. "Some other time, Billy." He ruffled the lad's hair. "I have to get back and see if the cadets are all right."

A few moments later Strong was speeding along the superhighway back toward the city. There was only one thing on his mind—to get the cadets out of the trap they were in. But it would be a hard job. Vidac had witnesses against them. He mentally probed the situation further. Why would Vidac abduct Professor Sykes? Surely not to frame the cadets. He must have wanted to be rid of Sykes too. Sykes must have known something. But what? Strong suddenly thought of the professor's investigation of the landing disturbance. It could only have been the result of radioactivity in a large mass. So the professor must have discovered a large deposit of uranium. Strong's mind raced on. Sykes would have taken the report to Vidac or Hardy, or both, and—

Strong forced himself to stop thinking. He was violating one of the cardinal laws of the Solar Alliance. He was presuming that Vidac or Hardy was guilty—and he didn't have an atom's worth of proof. There was only one way to get the proof. The cadets would have to escape to find it.

* * * * *

Strong sidled around the corner of the corridor. Down at the end of the hall, still standing in front of the cadet's door, Bush leaned against the wall, idly picking his teeth. Strong realized that he would have to sneak up behind the guard. He couldn't afford to be seen. He had to wait until Bush turned around.

He waited and watched while the man shifted from one foot to the other. And after what seemed like hours, Bush shifted his position and turned his back on the Solar Guard officer. Strong quickly darted around the corner and ran lightly down the hall. If Bush turned around now, Strong would be frozen stiff by the paralo ray. With ten feet to go, the captain lunged at Bush in a diving tackle, sending the man sprawling face forward. In a flash he was on top of him, and with a quick snapping blow on the back of the neck he knocked the man cold.

Strong snatched up the paralo-ray gun, then unlocked the door and threw it open. The cadets were sprawled on their bunks, listening to a story spool.

"Captain Strong!" yelled Tom.

"Quiet!" ordered Strong. "You've got three minutes. You'll find a jet car at the side entrance of the building. I can't explain now, but get out of here!"

"But what do you want us to do?" asked Tom. The three cadets were already grabbing their clothes and other items they would need.

"The only way you're going to prove that you didn't abduct or murder the professor is to find him," said Strong. "And pray to your stars that he's still alive. If he isn't, it'll be up to you to find out who killed him!"

"But what about you, sir?" asked Roger. "Won't Vidac know that you helped us?"

"Undoubtedly," said Strong. "After what I said to the guard today, Vidac will arrange for a hundred witnesses to prove that I helped you escape. You'll have to bring back the professor, not only to save your own necks, but my neck as well."

The three cadets nodded.

"All right," said Strong. "Spaceman's luck, and remember, you'll be wanted criminals when you walk out of that door. So act like criminals. Fight them the same way they will fight you. This is not a space maneuver. It's your lives against theirs!"

Without another word, the three cadets slipped out of the room and disappeared down the corridor.

Strong took a last look at Bush lying unconscious on the floor and hurried silently back to the front of the building. His heart was racing with excitement. The ball had begun to roll.

CHAPTER 17

"Where do we cut off?" asked Vidac. He sat beside Winters in the converted jet boat, speeding down the smooth highway that Strong had passed over only a few minutes before.

"It's right along here, somewhere," said Winters.

"Better slow down," said Vidac. "We don't want to miss it. We haven't much time. If Strong starts nosing around he might discover something."

"Lucky for us we found out so quickly where the uranium is," replied Winters.

"It won't mean a thing unless we can get Logan to sign over his land holdings."

Winters braked the jet car suddenly, throwing Vidac up against the windshield. "What are you doing?" snapped Vidac.

"Sorry, boss," replied Winters. "There's the road leading to the Logan place up ahead."

Winters slowed for the turn off the main highway and then accelerated to full power again on the side road.

"How are you going to get old Logan to sign the release?" asked Winters. "Suppose he knows his land is worth about ten billion credits?"

"How could he know?" asked Vidac. "The only ones that know are me, you, Bush, and Sykes."

Winters nodded. "Then as soon as we get Logan to sign over the land, we take care of Sykes, bring back his body as proof against the cadets, and everything's set, eh?"

"Something like that," said Vidac. "We still have to watch our step with Strong, though," said Vidac.

The two men were silent as the jet car raced down the side road. A moment later they could see the lights in the small crystal farmhouse.

"Cut your lights," said Vidac. "We don't want to scare them."

"O.K.," replied Winters. He switched off the powerful beams and slowed the car to a crawl. They rolled past the outer farm buildings and came to a stop in front of the main house.

"Say, boss," said Winters suddenly. "Look! Tracks in the road! Car tracks! Somebody's been out here! Logan doesn't have a car!"

"So what?" snarled Vidac. "Get hold of yourself. It could have been anyone."

A powerful light from the farmhouse suddenly flooded them and Logan's voice cracked in the night air.

"Who's there?" called the farmer.

"Good evening, Mr. Logan," said Vidac, climbing out of the car. "This is the governor."

"Vidac!" said Logan, startled. "What do you want?"

"This is what we want!" snarled Winters, whipping his ray gun into view. "Get back inside!"

"Wha—?" gasped Logan. "What's the meaning of this?"

"You'd better do as the man says, Mr. Logan," said Vidac.

Jane suddenly appeared behind Logan, her hands still soapy from washing the supper dishes. "Who is it, Father?" she asked, and then seeing Vidac and Winters she stepped back inside the house.

"Nothing to get alarmed about," said Vidac, pushing Logan into the house before him. "We just want to have a little talk." He smiled. "Business talk."

"Isn't it too bad, Winters," said Vidac, "that we just missed supper?"

"What do you want?" demanded Logan belligerently. He stepped in front of Jane protectively.

"Now don't get excited Mr. Logan," said Vidac, his voice smooth. "We just want you to sign a little paper, that's all."

"What kind of paper?" asked Logan.

"Say," said Winters suddenly, "ain't you got a kid?"

"If you mean my son, Billy," said Logan, "he's asleep."

"I'd better check," said Winters, starting forward.

"Never mind him," said Vidac. "We haven't got all night and there's nothing a kid could do."

He pulled out a paper from his pocket and unfolded it, keeping his eyes on Logan. "Mr. Logan, we're going to foreclose your mortgage."

"Foreclose!" gasped Logan. "But—but I haven't even had time to gather in my first crop!"

"We've taken a look at your fields and we don't think you're doing a good job," said Vidac. "In this mortgage you signed there's a clause that states I can foreclose any time I want."

"But how can you judge a crop by just looking at the fields?" asked Jane.

"Oh, we have ways, Miss Logan." Vidac smiled. He walked to a near-by table, and pushing a stack of study spools to the floor, spread the paper in front of him. He looked up at Logan and indicated the paper. "Do you have a pen, or would you like to use mine?"

"I'm not signing anything until I read it," snapped Logan.

Vidac smiled and pushed the paper across the table. Logan came forward and picked it up. He scanned it hurriedly and then glared at Vidac.

"You can't do this!" he snapped. "I won't sign!"

Winters suddenly leaped across the room and grabbed Jane by the wrist, jamming his gun in her back.

Vidac leered at the farmer. "Have you ever been frozen by a ray gun, Mr. Logan?"

Logan shook his head.

"Let me tell you about it," said Vidac coolly. "The effects are very simple, but very powerful. You are paralyzed! You can still see, hear, think, and breathe. Your heart continues to beat, but otherwise, you are absolutely powerless. The aftereffects are even worse. The person who has been frozen comes out completely whole, but"—Vidac suddenly shuddered—"believe me, Mr. Logan, you feel like ten thousand bells were vibrating in your brain at one time. It isn't pleasant!"

"Why—why—are you telling me this?" asked Logan.

"You wouldn't want to see your daughter undergo such an experience, would you?"

"If—if I sign the paper," stammered Logan, "will you leave Jane alone?"

"I give you my word as a spaceman that nothing will happen to her. In fact, when you sign, you will continue to work the farm as before. Only you'll be working for me. I wouldn't want to deprive you of your livelihood."

Suddenly the door to the bedroom opened and young Billy burst into the room, clad only in his pajamas.

"Don't sign, Pa!" he screamed. "Wait and tell Captain Strong first!"

"Strong!" exclaimed Vidac. "Has he been here?"

Logan nodded his head, and taking Vidac's pen, started to sign the paper.

"No—no, don't, Pa!" cried Billy. "Don't—!"

Logan paid no attention and finished signing. A look of deep hurt filled the boy's eyes. "A—a spaceman—" he stammered, "a Solar Guardsman would never have given up!" Crying, he turned away and buried his head in his sister's arms. Logan silently gave Vidac the paper and turned away.

"Thank you, Mr. Logan," said Vidac with a smile. "That's all. Good night!" He turned and motioned for Winters to follow him. "Come on. Let's get back to the city!"

Billy, Jane, and their father silently watched the two men leave the house. Even as the roar of the super-charged jet car faded away in the distance, they still stood in silence.

Finally Logan turned to his son and daughter. "There ain't but one thing left to do. Go back to Venus as soon as we can get passage. I'm sorry, Billy, but—"

"That's all right, Pa," said Billy. "I guess I would have done the same thing—for Jane."

* * * * *

"Can't you get any more out of this jalopy?" asked Roger.

Astro shook his head. "I've got her wide open now!"

The big cadet sat hunched over the steering wheel of the small jet car Strong had used a short time before, racing along the same smooth highway toward the spaceport on the other side of the hills. Tom was wedged in between Astro and Roger, his eyes straight ahead on the road.

"Where do we start first?" asked Roger.

"We've got to get a ship. The *Polaris*, if possible. We can't begin to look for the professor without one. As soon as Vidac learns that we've escaped, the whole satellite will be crawling with colonists and his boys, looking for us."

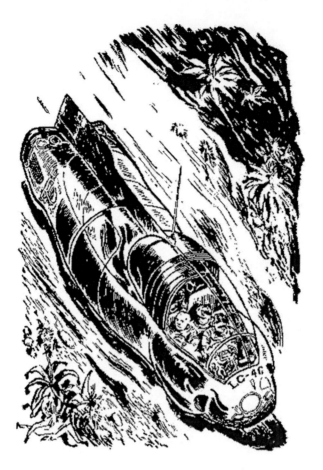

"We better take it easy, Astro," said Tom. "Turn off the lights."

"Colonists!" cried Astro. "Why would they want to help him?"

"Vidac will think of something to convince them that we're dangerous criminals," said Roger grimly. "Tom's right. We've got to get the *Polaris*."

They were just leaving the crystal city behind them and winding through the hill section surrounding the flat plain. Astro's handling of the jet car was perfect as he took the curves in the road at full throttle. They still had a long way to go to reach the spaceport that had been built on the other side of the hills.

"You sure did a fine job of conversion on these jet boats," said Tom to Astro. "This baby feels as though she was going to take off."

"I wish it was," said Roger, looking up at the hills on either side of them. "It would be a lot easier to blast over these things than go through them."

The car sped up to the last summit that separated them from the spaceport.

"We'd better take it easy," said Tom. "Turn off the lights, Astro. We'll ditch this jet car about a mile from the spaceport and walk the rest of the way."

"Right," said Astro. He gunned the little vehicle for the last burst of speed necessary to take them over the top. The jet car shuddered under the extra power and a moment later the spaceport lay spread before them. Below them, in a five-mile circle, they could see the few remaining ships of the great fleet. The *Polaris* was easily recognized, and fortunately, was on the nearer side of the giant landing area.

"There's home," said Roger.

"Yes," agreed Tom. "And she sure looks good to me—"

The curly-haired cadet suddenly stopped as powerful headlights loomed on the highway ahead.

"That's Vidac's jet car," said Roger. "I recognize the lights. We've got to get out of here!"

Astro braked the small vehicle and it screamed to a stop. The three cadets hastily piled out and raced for the darkness of the surrounding hills.

No sooner had they disappeared than Vidac's jet car slammed to a stop beside the deserted jet car. In a flash Vidac was out of the seat and examining the vehicle. He turned to Winters, holding a small disk in his hand. "Tom Corbett's identification tag!" said Vidac. "The cadets have escaped! Organize a search! The orders are *shoot to kill!*"

CHAPTER 18

Governor Hardy was not to be found. Strong made inquiries around the Administration Building and among the colonists but he could find no trace of the governor. The only thing Strong learned was that Hardy had spent the last two weeks wandering around in the outlying wilderness areas of the satellite, alone, apparently searching for something. But the Solar Guard captain realized that it would be a waste of time to race around the planet searching aimlessly for the governor. He became more and more convinced that Hardy was hiding. His suspicions were increased when he found Vidac waiting for him in the deserted lobby of the Administration Building with a warrant for his arrest. The warrant had been signed by Hardy.

"Before I place myself in your hands," said Strong, "I want to see the governor."

"Considering that you committed a crime by aiding the escape of the Space Cadets," said Vidac, "that will not be possible."

"I demand to see the governor!"

Vidac turned to Winters who was standing by his side. "Take him," he ordered.

Winters whipped out his paralo-ray gun, and before he could move, a paralyzing charge froze the Solar Guard captain in his tracks.

"Take him to my quarters," said Vidac. "And stay with him. I'm going to organize a searching party and find those cadets."

"Right," said Winters.

As Vidac walked away, Winters picked up the paralyzed body of the Solar Guard officer and carried him awkwardly to the slidestairs. Though under the effects of the paralo-ray, Strong's mind still continued to function. Even as Winters carried him across his shoulder like a stick of wood, Strong was planning his escape. He figured Winters would release him from the ray charge once inside Vidac's quarters and he was ready to go into action.

Winters opened the panel to Vidac's spacious office and carried Strong through to the other side where the lieutenant governor's sleeping quarters were located. He put the helpless man down on the bed, and stepping back to the panel, flipped on the neutralizer of the ray gun. He fired, releasing Strong from the frozen suspension.

Strong felt the jolts of the neutralizer charge but he clamped his teeth together to keep them from chattering and stayed rigid. He had to remain still, as if the neutralizer charge had not released him, in order to make his plan work. Winters waited for Strong to move, and when he didn't, stepped closer, prodding him with the barrel of the gun. In a flash Strong leaped up and grabbed the ray gun. Twisting it out of the surprised man's hand, he brought the weapon down on the man's neck. Winters dropped to the floor like a stone.

Then Strong scrambled to his feet and cold-bloodedly turned the ray on Winters, blasting him into immobility. He turned grimly toward the panel and raced to the slidestairs. If Vidac had a warrant for his arrest, signed by Hardy, then Vidac knew where Hardy was. If he could follow the lieutenant governor, he might possibly learn just where the mystery of Roald began and who was after what and why.

* * * * *

After leaving the jet car and climbing into the desolate hills surrounding Roald City, Tom, Roger, and Astro watched from the safety of a ridge the quick search Vidac and Winters had made to find them. When the two men had returned to the superhighway and blasted back toward the city, taking both jet cars, the three boys made their way slowly through the night down the opposite side of the hills and headed for the Logan farm. When the sun star rose over the satellite's horizon, the three boys were stretched out flat on their stomachs in a field, watching the morning activity of Jane, Billy, and Hyram Logan about the farm.

"Think we can get them to help us?" asked Roger.

"It's the only thing we can do," said Astro. "If they won't, we might as well give ourselves up. I'm so hungry I could eat a whole cow!"

"What kind of a cow?" asked Roger. "There aren't any on Roald, remember? We drink synthetic milk."

"I could even eat a synthetic cow!" was Astro's grim rejoinder.

"Come on, you two," said Tom. "We might as well try it. You think they're alone?"

"They don't act as though there's anyone around but themselves," said Roger. "But I don't know—"

"I thought I saw a curtain move at that window on the left a while ago," commented Astro, "and all three of them were outside."

"Probably a breeze," said Tom. "You cut over to the right, Astro. I'll go straight in, and you take the left, Roger. That way, if anything goes wrong, one or two of us might get away."

"All set?" asked Roger.

"Ready," nodded Astro.

"Let's go."

The three boys separated, and a moment later, when his unit mates were in position, Tom stood up and walked across the clearing, exposing himself to the house. Out of the corner of his eye he saw Astro and Roger moving in on the left and right. Billy was working in the front yard with his father, mixing chemicals. Jane was standing by the doorway of the house digging in a bed of flowers. Tom continued to walk right through the front yard and was only ten feet away from Billy before the youngster looked up.

"Tom!"

Logan turned and saw the cadet walking toward him. He stared. After a night scrambling around the hills, Tom looked as if he had been shoveling coal.

"Hello, Mr. Logan," said Tom, looking around. "Are you alone?"

"Yes," Logan replied. "Where are the other boys?"

"They're coming," said Tom, waving his arm toward his friends.

Astro and Roger rose from their places of concealment and darted forward.

"Get in the house, quick!" ordered Logan. "Vidac and his flunky Winters were out here last night and—" He didn't finish. The unmistakable roar of a jet car approaching rapidly was heard. The cadets raced for the house, following Jane into the farmer's bedroom, where they hid in a closet. Jane returned to the front of the house and stood with her father and Billy to watch the cloud of dust kicked up by the jet car as it raced along the dirt road toward them.

"If it's them space crawlers again," said Logan to his children, "let me do the talking."

"Who else could it be?" asked Jane.

"I don't know," said Logan. "But remember, if it is Vidac, we might be the only thing between those three boys inside and a long term on a prison rock!"

The jet car entered the cleared area in front of the house and stopped in a cloud of dust. Logan, grim-faced, followed by Billy and Jane walked across the yard to the car and waited. The door opened and a man in the uniform of an enlisted spaceman climbed out.

"Jeff Marshall!" yelled Billy.

"Hello, Mr. Logan, Jane, Billy." Jeff noticed the sudden look of relief that passed over Logan's face. "Is there something wrong?"

"Not a thing, Jeff," said Logan. "Come on in the house. We've got a surprise for you."

"Thank you, sir," said Jeff. "But I'm afraid I'm not in the mood for surprises. The cadets have escaped and the whole countryside is crawling with Vidac's men looking for them. There's a reward of a thousand credits for their capture—dead or alive!"

Logan patted the sergeant on the shoulder. "Stop worrying, Jeff. The cadets are in the house."

"What?"

Logan nodded his head. "Come on inside." He paused and spoke to his son. "Billy, you scoot down the road to the bend and watch the main highway. If anyone turns off into our road, you let me know right away!"

"Yes, sir," replied Billy and dashed down the road. Jeff followed Jane and Logan into the house, and a few moments later, after exchanging enthusiastic greetings, he and the cadets waited hungrily for Jane to prepare breakfast.

Finishing the hearty meal in short order and sipping hot bracing coffee, the three cadets took turns in telling Jeff of their conversations with Strong, their escape, and their near encounter with Vidac on the highway the night before.

"What made you come out here, Jeff?" Tom finally asked.

"Well, when I discovered that you had escaped, I knew you'd head for one of two places, the spaceport or here. I hung around the spaceport all night waiting for you to show up, and when you didn't, I came here."

"That's dangerous," said Logan. "If you figured it that way, Vidac can do the same thing. I wouldn't want him to find you boys here. Not that I don't want to help you, but Vidac might try to connect me with you and the missing professor. I couldn't take a risk like that with Billy and Jane. We're in enough trouble."

The farmer then told them how Vidac had forced him to sign a release on his land while threatening Jane with a ray gun.

"We have to get to the bottom of this mess," said Tom. "The only trouble is we don't know what he's after or why he's trying to frame us."

"Well," said Roger, glancing at his watch, "whatever we decide, we'd better do it quickly. It's almost noon."

"Noon!" exclaimed Logan. "Why it can't be more than nine at the most!" He pulled out a large gold watch from his coverall pocket. "Sure—it's a quarter to nine!"

Jeff looked at his watch. "Same here!" He smiled. "You must be wrong, Roger."

"You probably forgot to wind it," said Tom. He glanced casually at his own watch and suddenly exclaimed. "Say, my watch has three-thirty!"

"And mine says four twenty-two!" cried Astro.

Roger and Tom looked at each other, eyes widening.

"You don't think—?" began Tom, hardly daring to breathe.

"Yes, I do!" said Roger. "Remember what happened to the instruments?"

"Uranium!" exclaimed Astro.

The word echoed in the kitchen like the blast of a bomb. The boys looked at each other, too startled to explain to Logan and Jane, who, though they were listening intently, were unable to fathom the boys' reasoning.

"Where were you last night?" asked Jeff quickly.

Roger described as nearly as he could remember the exact route that they had traveled in making their way to the Logan farm.

"Hey, I think I've got the answer, fellows!" Tom suddenly exclaimed. "If Vidac came out here last night and took over Mr. Logan's farm, and we're falsely accused of getting rid of the professor, and the professor is missing, there must be something to tie it all together. Vidac wouldn't do the things he's done, unless he's got a rocket-blasting good reason!"

Roger quickly added, "And he wouldn't try to buck Captain Strong unless he was playing for high stakes!"

"Right," said Tom. "The only thing that could have caused our watches to go haywire, like the ships instruments, would be uranium. Lots of uranium. And uranium is the only thing valuable enough to make Vidac take such long chances."

"But how can you tell it's uranium?" asked Logan.

"Our watches are not ordinary timepieces, sir," explained Tom. "They are specially constructed for use in space travel. Each watch is electrically controlled and highly sensitive."

"Electric?" repeated Logan in amazement. "Electric wrist watches? That small thing?"

Tom smiled. "Each is charged by a miniature power pack, sir."

"The uranium deposits out in the hills affected these watches," continued Astro, "the same way they affected the electronic instruments on the spaceships coming in to Roald."

"I'll tell you what," said Jeff. "I'll make a check."

"Wait a minute," said Logan. "I just remembered something—"

"What, sir?" asked Tom.

"Professor Sykes! He was out here poking around in my fields and up in the hills from dawn till dark. Said he was making some soil tests. I yelled at him for stepping all over some baby fruit trees."

"That's it, then," said Roger grimly. "This area is jumping with uranium and Vidac now has title to the land!"

"Don't be so sure," said Tom. "We still need proof."

"Isn't using force to take the land away proof enough?" snapped Logan.

"Wait a minute!" said Jeff. "If you want proof, I know where to get it."

"Where?" asked Tom.

"The professor's work journal!"

"Think he'd record it in there?" asked Tom. "It's pretty valuable information."

"Yes," said Jeff. "He even logs the amount of coffee he drinks in the morning! He puts down everything!"

"You think the journal is still in the lab?" asked Tom.

"Sure it is. I saw it before I left."

"Then we've got Vidac right where we want him!" exclaimed Roger.

"No, we haven't," said Tom. "We haven't got the professor to prove it! Vidac's still the boss on this hunk of space rock, and we're still wanted for murder!"

The door burst open and Billy raced into the room. "A jet car just turned off the highway! It's coming here!"

"We've got to get out of here!" said Tom. He turned to Jeff. "If it's Vidac, tell him you've come to take Jane out on a date. That should explain your presence. Then get the professor's journal and give it to Captain Strong. He'll know what to do!"

Roger and Astro were cramming food in their pockets. "Come on, Tom," said Roger. "I can hear the jets."

"What are you boys going to do?" asked Jane.

"Try to get to the *Polaris*," replied Tom. "Then we'll hunt for the professor. If we don't find him, we're sunk. He's the key to the whole thing."

Astro and Roger had tumbled out the window and were racing toward the safety of the near-by hills. Tom gave Jeff a final handshake and dived out the window after them. Running toward the clump of bushes where Astro and Roger had just disappeared, he dived for cover, just as Vidac's car roared into the clearing. The boys saw Vidac and Bush get out of the car, and after inspecting Jeff's, turn and stride into the house.

"Come on," said Tom. "We've got to get to the *Polaris!*"

The three boys turned away and hurried from the farm. In a few minutes, after scrambling to the top of the nearest hill, they turned back to look down on the farmhouse and saw Jeff escorting Jane to his car.

"So far so good," said Tom. "Let's go."

They walked off and were soon lost in the tangle of scrub grass and dry gullies, their destination the *Polaris* and the solution to the mystery of Professor Sykes's disappearance.

CHAPTER 19

Strong's plan to follow Vidac in order to locate Hardy had paid off. While Vidac and Bush were rounding up citizens of Roald City and sending them out to search for the Space Cadets, the Solar Guard captain had checked the frequency setting on the communicator in the lieutenant governor's jet car. Then hiding in Professor Sykes's laboratory, Strong tuned the lab communicator to the same frequency and waited. He knew he was taking a chance. Vidac might not contact the governor on that setting if he contacted the governor at all, but there was no other way at the moment. Strong waited three hours before hearing the click of Vidac's communicator on the laboratory speaker.

"Able One to Able Two. Can you hear me, Able Two? Come in, Able Two!" Vidac's voice crackled through the set.

Strong listened intently and was rewarded by the sound of another click and another voice speaking.

"Able Two to Able One. Come in."

"I've got Strong," reported Vidac, "and the cadets are somewhere in the hills between here and the spaceport. I've just organized the colonists into searching parties and am about to leave."

"Good. Contact me the minute you find them."

"Right. Keep an eye out for them. They might try to reach the spaceport."

"Very well. I've set up an alarm on the outer hatch. No one can get aboard without my knowing it."

"Right. Able One out."

"Able Two out."

Strong heard the clicks of the two communicators and sat back, breathing hard. He had recognized the voice of Able Two instantly. It was Governor Hardy. He was at the spaceport, hiding aboard a spaceship. But why? Could he be mixed up in this affair?

Pacing the floor restlessly, Strong tried to figure out the connection. Hardy's reputation was spotless. It seemed inconceivable that he could be involved with Vidac. And yet Hardy had selected Vidac as his right-hand man. And Vidac couldn't have gotten away with his treatment of the colonists unless Hardy had silently endorsed his orders.

The Solar Guard captain left the laboratory and watched the colonists as they milled around in front of the Administration Building. Vidac's jet car was in the middle of the group of men and Strong saw him jump up on top of the car and begin addressing them. He couldn't hear the lieutenant governor's words, but he knew the men were being urged to hunt the cadets down like common criminals. He watched until Vidac rocketed off in his jet car, followed by a stream of colonists in various types of vehicles. In a few moments the area in front of the Administration Building was quiet and deserted. Strong began searching for a jet car.

* * * * *

Jeff Marshall turned sideways in his seat and looked at the pretty face of Jane Logan. Her brow was furrowed with worry.

"Are you afraid?" asked Jeff as he guided the car down the private road leading to the highway.

"I'm frightened to death!" murmured Jane. "That man Vidac is so ruthless!"

Jeff grunted. "I have to agree with you there. But Tom is right. We need proof before we can stop him."

The girl shrank back. As far as one could see, the road was lined with jet cars. Colonists with paralo-ray guns and anything that could be used as a weapon were scrambling around in the hills.

"What does it mean?" asked Jane.

"I don't know," replied Jeff. "But I think it's a search for the cadets!"

"Oh, no!" cried Jane.

"I hope they'll let us through," said Jeff. He pressed down on the accelerator and started moving along the line of cars. On either side of the highway, he saw colonists beating the bushes, looking behind rocks and boulders, shouting at each other as they pressed their hunt for Astro, Tom, and Roger. Jeff managed to get halfway past the line of cars when ahead of him another jet car pulled out across the highway, blocking it. He was forced to stop.

"Hold on there!" roared a man suddenly appearing at the side of the car, holding a paralo-ray gun pointed directly at Jeff.

Jeff looked at him in mock surprise. "What's going on here?" he asked.

"Who are you?" demanded the man roughly.

"Jeff Marshall. And this is Jane Logan. What's all the fuss about?"

"We're looking for the Space Cadets. They murdered old Professor Sykes!" snapped the man. His eyes narrowed and he looked at Jeff closely. "You were pretty chummy with them, weren't you?" he asked.

"Sure, I knew them," replied Jeff calmly. "But if they've done anything to the professor, I want them caught as badly as you do. I've been the professor's assistant for years. He's—he's like a father to me."

Several of the other men had gathered around the car and were listening. "That's right, Joe," said a man on the outside of the group. "This feller's okay. And that's Logan's daughter, all right. They ain't done nothing."

"When was the last time you saw the cadets?" demanded the man called Joe.

"Why, a couple of days ago," Jeff replied.

There was a long pause while the man continued to look at Jeff ominously. Finally he stepped back and lowered the paralo-ray gun. "All right, go on. But if you see those murdering cadets, let us know. We're out to get them, and when we do, we're going to—"

"But what right have you to do this on your own?" cried Jane.

"We ain't," said Joe. "Governor Vidac made us all special deputies this morning."

"But we'd do it, anyway," cried someone from the rear of the crowd. "Those Space Cadets are guilty and we're going to see that they get what's coming to them!" There was a roar of agreement.

Jeff nodded, stepped on the accelerator, and eased the car slowly through the group of men. As soon as he was free, he stepped down hard and sent the jet car racing along the highway back toward Roald City.

"Jeff—Jeff," asked Jane despairingly, "do you think they'll catch the boys?"

"I don't know," replied Jeff grimly. "But if they are caught, the only way we can save them is to find the professor's journal and pray that the uranium report is in it."

"But you said the information would be there," said Jane.

"When you need something as badly as we need that report," replied Jeff, "you never find it."

* * * * *

The three Space Cadets were watching their pursuers from a high ridge. They had been driven back all day, and now they could go no farther. Caught while climbing down the other side of the hills from the Logan farm, they had narrowly escaped detection at the very beginning and had been racing from cover to cover ever since. Now there was no place to go. It was only a question of time before the colonists would reach the top of the ridge and find them.

"What do you think they'll do?" asked Roger.

"We'll be sent off this satellite so fast," answered Tom, "you'll get sick from acceleration."

"Why?" asked Astro.

"Vidac won't want us hanging around. Not since Captain Strong is here. He'll give us a trial within an hour, sentence us to life on a prison rock, and delegate some of his boys to take us back. We don't have a chance."

Astro let out a low animal-like growl. "If that happens," said the giant Venusian, "I'll get off that rock someway, somehow. And I'll find Mr. Vidac. And when I do—"

"No need to talk like that now," said Tom. "Let's just not get caught!"

"But how?" asked Roger. "Look, over there! They've already reached the top of that ridge on the left. The party on the right will be up there soon too. We're trapped!"

"Wait a minute," said Astro. He picked up a huge boulder and hefted it in his arms. "We can stand them off all day by tumbling rocks down on them."

"And kill innocent people who don't know what they're doing?" asked Tom. "No—put it down, Astro!"

"All right, brains!" snapped Roger. "What have you got to suggest?"

"There's only one thing we can do!" said Tom. "Down on the side of the hill here I noticed a small cave. Two of us could squeeze inside."

"Why only two?" asked Astro.

"Somebody would have to cover the entrance from the outside with a boulder and then give himself up!"

Astro slapped Tom on the back. "That's a terrific idea. Come on. You two hide and I'll move the rock over."

"Wait a minute, you goof," said Roger. "Don't be in such a hurry to be a blasted hero!" He turned to Tom. "Just like that Venusian hick to be ready to sacrifice himself to get a Solar Medal!"

"Don't argue, Junior," snapped Astro. "I'm the only one strong enough to move one of those rocks. You two hide and I'll cover you."

"Now wait a minute, Astro," Tom protested. "I didn't mean . . ."

"You should have," replied Astro. "And if you don't get moving now, you'll never make it!"

Roger looked at Tom and nodded. "Guess he's right for once in his life, Tom. He's the only one strong enough to do it."

Tom hesitated and then slapped Astro on the back. "All right, Astro," he said. "But there's more to it than just giving yourself up! You've got to make them think that Roger and I ran out on you. That way they'll continue to search for us, but in another direction. And Vidac won't try to do anything to you alone. He'll wait until he's got all of us."

"O.K.," said Astro. "I get it. Come on. Get in that cave."

The three boys scrambled down the side of the hill and found the cave Tom had seen. After a quick search Astro found a boulder that half-covered the front of the cave, and the three boys pushed it close to the entrance.

"Go on. Get inside now," said Astro. "I'll push this one into position and then pile a few smaller ones on top and around it. That way you'll be able to get air and still be hidden."

Tom and Roger crawled into the hole and settled themselves as Astro pushed the boulder up against the opening. He piled the other stones around it quickly. When he had just about finished he heard someone behind him. He turned and saw one of the colonists scrambling down the side of the hill, heading for him.

"Here they come," Astro whispered hoarsely. "Spaceman's luck!" He dropped the last stone in place and turned to face the man who was now almost upon him.

Tom and Roger crouched in the darkness and listened intently.

"You there!" they heard the colonist cry. "Halt! Don't move or I'll freeze you!"

Astro stood still. The man came up to him and felt the cadet's uniform for a hidden weapon. Then he jammed the ray gun into Astro's back and ordered him down the hill. Astro started walking, hardly daring to breathe, but suddenly the man stopped.

"Where are the others?" he demanded.

"They ran out on me."

"Ran out on you. I thought you three were supposed to be such good buddies?"

"When the chips were down," said Astro as harshly as he could, "they turned out to be nothing but yellow rats!"

"Which way did they go?"

"I don't know," said Astro. "It happened last night. We went to sleep, and when I woke up, they were gone."

"Where'd they go?" snarled the man, pushing the ray gun into Astro's back.

"I—I—" Astro pretended he didn't want to talk.

"I'll freeze you, so help me," said the man. "I'm going to count five—one, two, three, four—"

"Don't! I'll tell you!" cried Astro. "I'm not sure, but I think they headed back for the city. We were talking about it last night. We figured it would be the best place to hide."

"Ummm. That makes sense," said the man. "I guess you're telling the truth. Now get down the hill. One false move and I'll blast you!"

Astro turned and stumbled down the hill in front of the paralo-ray gun. A smile tugged at his lips.

Vidac and Bush were waiting for them on the highway at the bottom of the hill.

"Where are Corbett and Manning?" Vidac demanded, looking at Astro.

Astro repeated the story about Tom and Roger having deserted him.

Vidac eyed him speculatively. "They just walked out on you?" he asked.

Astro nodded.

Vidac turned to the colonists who were standing around listening to the giant Venusian's story. "All right, men," he said, "I guess he's telling the truth. Back to the city. There aren't too many places they could be hiding."

The men turned and ran for their cars. Vidac continued to look at Astro, a thin smile tugging at his lips, his eyes twinkling. "You stay here with me, Bush," said Vidac.

"But you said—"

"Never mind what I said," snapped Vidac. "I'm telling you to stay here. Have some of the colonists double up and leave a jet car here."

In a few moments the rest of the jet cars were roaring off toward the city. Vidac waited until the last car had vanished down the road, then he turned to Astro, "Do you really think you fooled me with that stuff about Manning and Corbett running out on you?"

"What happened to them then?" asked Astro innocently.

"We'll see," said Vidac softly, looking up into the hills.

Holding a paralo-ray gun on the giant cadet, Vidac forced him into his jet car. Bush slid under the wheel and started the jets.

"You think the cadets are still up there in the hills?" asked Bush.

"Never mind what I think," snapped Vidac. "Head for the spaceport."

Vidac spun around in his seat and looked back along the highway. He punched Astro in the shoulder and motioned for him to look. Astro turned to see the jet car left by Vidac pulling away from the hills.

"They must have heard every word I said," mused Vidac. He turned to Bush. "When they reach the spaceport, don't bother waiting for them to get out of the car. Blast them on sight!"

"What are you going to do?" asked Astro tightly.

"Don't you remember your Space Code laws, Astro?" asked Vidac. "Article Sixteen? It specifically states that in cases of emergency, the commanding officer of a Solar Guard community can be the judge and jury, and can pass sentence for felonies or worse. In two hours you and your buddies will be aboard the *Polaris*, under guard, and headed for a life sentence on a prison rock!" He laughed. "And I'll make it stick!"

CHAPTER 20

Jeff Marshall was just turning the jet car into the Plaza in front of the Administration Building when Jane suddenly grabbed his arm.

"Jeff, look!" she cried. "Isn't that Captain Strong?"

The enlisted spaceman slowed the car and followed the direction of Jane's pointing finger. He saw Strong step around the corner of the Administration Building, stop, then scurry back around to the side. The streets of the city were deserted. "He's running away from us," said Jeff. "Probably thinks we're part of that searching party coming back."

He brought the car to a screaming halt in front of the building and jumped out, calling, "Captain Strong!" His voice echoed through the deserted streets. "This is Jeff Marshall!"

Peering around the corner of the Administration Building, Strong saw Marshall clearly and then recognized the daughter of Hyram Logan. He dashed out of his hiding place and greeted them with a yell.

"Jeff! Jeff! Over here!"

The three friends of the Space Cadets were soon telling each other the latest developments. Strong listened to Jeff's story of the professor's work journal and shook his head disgustedly. "I was in that lab for nearly four hours this morning," he said. "If I had only known."

"Don't blame yourself, sir," said Jeff. "You didn't know it was there!"

"Let's find it now," said Jane desperately. "We're losing time. Those men back in the hills may catch the boys."

"They haven't been caught yet," asserted Strong. "And if I know my cadets, those men will have a hard time nailing them.

Come on!" He turned and raced into the Administration Building, heading for Professor Sykes's laboratory.

In less than five minutes Jeff was searching through the pages of the professor's work journal. "There's no telling when he made the discovery," said Jeff, scanning the mass of complicated diagrams and figures.

"It must have been soon after our arrival on Roald," said Jane. "That was when we saw him searching the hills around our farm."

Jeff flipped the pages back to the front of the book and began to read it from the beginning. "Here's something!" He quoted some figures from the book and looked at Strong.

"That make any sense to you, sir?" he asked.

"It sure does!" said Strong. "That's a preliminary survey on uranium! He's just getting the scent there. Keep reading."

Jeff turned a few more pages and suddenly stopped. "Here it is!" he exclaimed. "And say—look at this!" He handed the journal over to Strong who began to read quickly. "' . . . conclusive proof found today in hills surrounding farming area of Hyram Logan. Potentially the biggest hot metal strike I've ever seen. Am going to make a report to Vidac today. This could mean the beginning of a new era in space travel. Enough fuel to send fleets of ships on protracted voyages to any part of the universe . . . '"

Strong stopped reading and looked at Jane and Jeff.

"This was dated the tenth." He turned the page and continued, "This is the day after, the eleventh. Listen to this! ' . . . Vidac is sending my information to the Solar Council immediately. He was very impressed.' And so forth and so forth."

Strong closed the journal and faced Jeff and Jane again, a triumphant smile on his lips. "This is just what we needed. This journal is admissible in Solar Courts as evidence the same way a ship's log is! Come on. Now we've got to get Vidac before he gets the cadets!"

"Wait," said Jane in a fearful whisper. "Listen."

Strong and Jeff stood still. In the distance they heard the unmistakable roar of jet cars converging on the Plaza. Strong turned to Jeff. "They've either found the cadets or—"

"Or what?" asked Jeff.

"I—I won't say it," said Strong hesitantly, "but if anything has happened to those boys, I'll personally dig Vidac's grave!"

Jane had moved to the window and was watching the wild activity in the Plaza below. "They're spreading out!" she cried. "They must be searching the city."

Strong rushed to the window and looked down. "That means they haven't found the cadets!" he exclaimed.

"I've been thinking, sir," said Jeff. "Do you think we really have enough proof of Vidac's guilt to make the colonists understand it was Vidac and not the cadets who could have done something to the professor?"

"We've got to try!" said Strong. "We've got to try!"

The two spacemen and Jane left the laboratory and raced down the slidestairs and through the halls of the Administration Building to the double doors that opened onto the Plaza. They stepped into view just as the colonists were about to spread out and search the city. One of the men was standing on the steps shouting orders. Jeff recognized him as Joe, the man who had stopped him on the highway. There was a roar from the crowd when they noticed Strong, Jeff, and Jane standing in the open doorway.

Strong held the black journal high over his head and called for order. The colonists crowded around at the base of the steps not knowing what to make of his sudden appearance.

"What are you doing here?" demanded the colonist deputy. "You're Captain Strong of the Solar Guard, aren't you?"

"That's right," replied Strong. "And you're making a big mistake accusing the cadets of the murder of Professor Sykes, when you're not even sure the professor has been murdered! The man you want to question about that is Lieutenant Governor Vidac!"

A startled murmur ran through the assembled men. Strong continued, "I have absolute proof that Vidac received information about the biggest uranium strike in the history of the universe from Professor Sykes and plans to keep it for himself. His accusation of the cadets is a cover-up to clear himself and to throw you off the track."

The word *uranium* spread through the crowd like wildfire.

"You're pretty friendly with the cadets," sneered the deputy. "How do we know you're telling us the truth, and not just trying to save them?"

"Yeah. Answer that one!" roared a voice from back of the crowd.

"Do any of you understand physics?" asked Strong.

"Physics?" asked the deputy. "What's that got to do with it?"

"Plenty! I have information here in this journal that will prove what I just said! Read it for yourself. It's in the professor's own handwriting."

"I can read it," said a small man in front of Strong. "Gimme that thing!" Strong handed him the black book and told the man where to look. The man considered it for five minutes, then turned to the crowd. "He's right! We're sitting on the hottest uranium rock in this galaxy!"

"Where is it?" cried someone from the crowd. "Tell us where the uranium is!"

The mob of men, forgetting all about the cadets, were now seized with the greed for riches. Strong took the journal back and tucked it under his arm.

"I'll tell you where it is," said Strong, "when we put Vidac where he belongs! Behind bars!"

"What are we waiting for?" cried the colonists. "Let's get that murdering space crawler!"

The deputy pushed his way through the crowd and raced for his car. Others followed and once more the Plaza echoed to the roar of jets.

Strong turned to Jeff. "You'll find Winters up in Vidac's quarters. I had to freeze him." He handed over the paralo-ray gun. "Get him and follow us to the spaceport. Tell him we know everything, and if he doesn't talk, he'll get life on a prison rock."

"Right," said Jeff. "I'll get a confession out of him if I have to wring his neck—and I'll get it on a soundscriber!"

"Good. Come on, Jane," said Strong. "This is the finish of a would-be tyrant!"

Jeff turned and dashed back into the building, while Strong and Jane climbed into the jet car and roared off toward the spaceport.

"If we only had a paralo-ray gun," muttered Roger as he and Tom sped after Vidac's powerful jet car.

"Yes," agreed Tom. "This could be a trap, but what can we do?"

Roger was silent. They had moved out of the cave as soon as Astro had been taken down the hill and they knew exactly what Vidac had in mind. But their need for information about Professor

Sykes and their concern for Astro forced them to follow the powerful jet car into what they were certain was a trap.

"We'll ditch the jet car after we find out where they're going," said Tom, "and figure out something afterward."

"You think they'll go to Sykes?" asked Roger.

"It's a pretty safe bet, Roger. The professor's been well hidden, so why not hide Astro in the same place, hoping in the meantime to get us also."

"But I can't see walking into a trap, simply because we know it's there!"

"Roger—look! Vidac's stopping the car! Astro's trying to get away!"

"Astro's fighting with Bush!" shouted Roger. "Come on! Can't you get any more push out of this wagon?"

Tom jammed the accelerator down to the floorboard and the jet car fairly leaped ahead. Fifty yards from Vidac's stalled car, Tom slammed on the brake, bringing the little car to a screaming halt only two feet away. Roger was halfway out before the car had stopped moving. Beside Vidac's car, Bush was wrestling with Astro.

"Tom! Roger! Get back! It's a trap!" yelled Astro.

Astro's warning came too late. While Tom and Roger sprang to help their unit mate, Vidac slipped up on the other side and fired quickly and accurately with a paralo-ray gun. Tom and Roger were frozen just as they were about to pull Bush from Astro's back.

Vidac swung the ray gun around toward Astro. "See that, big boy?" He laughed. "Well, you're going to get the same thing if you make one funny move. Now pile those two stiffs into the back of my car! Get moving!"

Seething with frustration and rage, Astro turned to Roger and Tom, standing like solid slabs of stone. He picked up Roger and carried him gently to the car, placing him in the back. Then he turned and walked toward Tom. He made a slight movement toward Vidac and Bush, but they leveled their guns quickly.

"None of that," warned Vidac. Astro's shoulders drooped. He was almost in tears as he walked toward Tom. The curly-haired cadet stood immovable, staring at his friend. The Venusian leaned over and picked up Tom gently.

"Take it easy, Astro," whispered Tom, not moving his lips. "I'm not frozen. He missed me!"

Astro nearly jumped at the sound of Tom's voice. He recovered quickly, fighting back a grin of triumph. He threw a quick glance at Vidac and Bush, then carefully picked Tom up and carried him to the car. As he was about to turn around again, he felt the sudden jolt of the paralo ray, and in the split-second before the ray took effect, Astro nearly laughed.

* * * * *

Under the effects of a paralo-ray charge the body is paralyzed and there is no feeling. Tom, however, lying beside Roger but beneath Astro in the back seat of the car, began to suffer painful muscular cramps. He gritted his teeth, trying to lie rigidly still, but his arms and legs began to jerk spasmodically and he had to move.

Slowly he eased one arm from beneath Astro's heavy body and shifted his legs into a more comfortable position. Though the Venusian's weight still pressed him down in the seat, the muscular cramps were relieved. He began to pay attention to what Vidac and Bush were saying in the front seat of the car.

"We'll blast off as soon as we reach the spaceport," said Vidac, "and get up to the asteroid."

"Why so fast?" asked Bush.

"I want to get rid of those nosy space rats as quickly as possible. Then I'll go after Strong."

Bush shook his head. "That won't be easy. Strong's not a Space Cadet. He's Solar Guard. And good Solar Guard at that!"

Tom smiled in wholehearted agreement with the lieutenant governor's henchman.

Vidac sneered. "Don't make me laugh! Didn't you see the way I convinced those dumb colonists that the cadets were responsible for the professor's murder? If they'd stopped to think about it, they would have realized I was putting one over on them. All you have to do is keep talking, fast and loud. Keep them off balance, and don't let them think."

"There's the spaceport road," said Bush. "And there's the *Polaris*. I hope we don't have any trouble with the grease monkeys when they see us hauling the cadets out."

"If they start anything," said Vidac with a sneer, "you know what to do."

"Sure," said Bush, patting his paralo-ray gun.

The car roared through the gates of the spaceport and sped across the hard surface of the field. A moment later it came to a shuddering stop at the base of the giant rocket cruiser.

"All right," said Vidac. "Get them aboard the ship. Hardy will blow a gasket if we don't get this over with in a hurry."

Hardy! The name hit Tom like a trip hammer. So Hardy was mixed up in it! Hardy, the respected Governor of Roald, the man responsible for the welfare of the colony and the lives of the colonists, was really a swindler and a thief. Now if Jeff only had Professor Sykes's journal they could tie everything together, providing he could stop Vidac from sending them off to a prison rock! Tom's thoughts were suddenly interrupted by the movement of Astro's heavy body on top of him. The young cadet broke out into a cold sweat. When he had been supposedly hit by the paralo ray his arms had been outstretched! He had been so busy thinking about Hardy's connection with Vidac that he had forgotten to resume his original position.

Astro was hauled out of the car and Bush reached in the car to get Tom. The boy braced himself and waited as the spaceman grabbed him by the feet. He was pulled roughly out of the door and stood on his feet. Out of the corner of his eye he could see that Astro had been stood up beside the car like a tree. Vidac turned away from the giant cadet and started to give Bush a hand. Suddenly he stopped and pulled out his paralo-ray gun.

"Boss, what're you doing?" cried Bush, jumping away from Tom and leaving the cadet rocking on his feet, trying to pretend he was still paralyzed. He toppled forward, and before he realized what he had done, threw out his hands to break his fall.

Vidac laughed. "I have to hand it to you, Corbett. That was the best bit of acting I've ever seen in my life."

Tom picked himself up from the ground and glared at Vidac. Bush stood to one side, too startled to realize what had happened.

"You mean, he—he—" Bush stammered, his eyes wide with alarm.

"That's right," said Vidac. "The wonder boy of the space lanes acted as if he was frozen. What were you going to do, Corbett? Take over, maybe?"

"You'll never get away with it, Vidac," said Tom through clenched teeth. "You're through and you know it!"

"Not yet, my friend," said Vidac. "You've had your fun. Now get your friend out of the car and carry him aboard the *Polaris*. We're all going for a little ride!"

Tom turned reluctantly and began pulling Roger out of the back of the car. He realized that he could take no more chances with the paralo ray. As long as he was awake, there was a chance for him to do something. He lifted Roger gently to his shoulder, turned, and staggered toward the cruiser. Just as he was about to step inside the hatch, he heard the faint roar of jets in the distance. He stumbled and fell purposely to stall for time. He and Roger sprawled full length on the deck. As Tom sat up and rubbed his knee, Bush rushed over, leaving Vidac to struggle with the immense bulk of Astro.

"Get up!" snarled Bush. He poked the gun within an inch of Tom's face. The cadet knew that if Bush fired at such a close range, his brains would be burned to a crisp. He fell away from the gun.

"I wrenched my knee," he whined. "I can't get up!"

"If you don't get up by the time I count three," growled Bush, "I'll blast you! One, two—"

The roar of the jets was closer now and Tom's heart began to race. Feigning pain in his leg, he started to pull himself to his feet. He glanced toward the spaceport entrance and saw a stream of jet cars pouring into the field, heading for the *Polaris*. Suddenly Tom leaped for Bush from the crouching position. He lashed out with his right fist, while grabbing for the ray gun with his left.

Bush was not to be tricked so easily. He fired just as the cadet jumped. But in trying to evade Tom's crashing right hand, he missed his shot and was grazed by Tom's fist. He fell back out of the spaceship, his gun falling inside the air-lock portal.

Tom lay on the deck, wincing in pain. The wild shot had caught him in the right leg and he was unable to move it. He crawled across the deck, reaching for the gun as Bush came charging up the ramp.

Meanwhile, Vidac, seeing the commotion in the hatch of the spaceship, pulled his gun and leveled it at Tom. But Bush charged through the hatch just as Vidac fired and he caught the full blast of Vidac's shot. He landed on the deck beside Tom, stiff as a board.

Tom reached for the gun, preparing to fight it out with Vidac. But the odds were against him. His leg was completely paralyzed and Vidac was climbing into the ship. He knew he couldn't reach the gun in time.

Suddenly Vidac became aware of the jet cars streaming into the spaceport. He stopped and turned to look at them. Then, sensing something was wrong, he turned back to dash into the *Polaris*. The second his back was turned was sufficient time for Tom to grab the gun and fire. Vidac was stopped cold, his bright eyes burning with hate, unable to move.

"You can drop that now," said a voice in back of Tom.

The curly-haired cadet whirled around to face Governor Hardy, holding a paralo-ray rifle up to his shoulder, aimed and ready to fire.

"You're a good spaceman, Corbett," said Hardy in a cold, harsh voice, "but this is the last time you'll ever get into my hair!"

Tom's leg prevented him from moving and he had turned in an awkward sitting position to face Hardy. All he could do was bring his gun up quickly and fire over his left shoulder. Hardy fired at the same instant. At such close range neither could miss.

When Captain Strong and the colonists dashed into the ship they found two perfect statues.

CHAPTER 21

"And you kept giving Hardy wrong information?" asked Strong with a laugh.

"Yes!" snorted Professor Sykes with a wry grin. "You see, I knew right away Vidac was doing something funny way back—" He paused to sip his tea. "Way back before we landed on Roald." He grinned broadly at the people seated around the table in the dining room of the Logan house, Roger, Astro, Jeff, Tom, Jane, Billy, Hyram, and Strong.

After Strong had released the Space Cadets from the effects of the paralo rays, they had searched the *Polaris* and found the professor locked in one of the cabins. Placing Vidac and Hardy under arrest and confining them in the brig of the ship with Winters and Bush, they had returned to the Logan farm to clear a few of the mysteries surrounding the nightmare of violence since their landing on Roald.

"When Vidac and Hardy refused to let me go down and make an inspection of the satellite after the instruments conked out, I knew there was something fishy," Sykes continued. "Any fool could have seen that radioactivity would be the only thing to cause an instrument disturbance like that!"

"Then Vidac and Hardy knew about the uranium?" asked Strong. "We only discovered it at Space Academy ourselves a little while ago."

"They knew about it all right," asserted Sykes. "Hardy told me so himself. He got the information from an old prospector who had made application to come to Roald as a colonist. The space rat had been here before, as a sailor on a deep spacer that had wandered off course. The ship was running low on water so the skipper sent him down to the satellite to see if he could find any. He found the water and the uranium too. But he clammed up about that, hoping to keep it a secret until he could go back and claim it. His only chance was to become a colonist, and when he washed out in the screening, he told Hardy, hoping to bribe his way. Of course Hardy double-crossed him to get the uranium himself. That was why you were pulled off the project and sent to Pluto, Strong. Then he got Vidac to be his aide and everything looked rosy."

"It's still hard to believe that Hardy was behind the whole operation," said Astro, shaking his head. "Imagine—the governor of the colony ratting on his own people."

"It's happened before, unfortunately," commented Strong. "Better men than Hardy have succumbed to the lure of riches and power."

"You're right, Strong," snapped Sykes. "That's just what happened to Hardy. While I was his prisoner on the *Polaris*, he kept boasting about how rich he was going to be—how powerful. When I reminded him of his past achievements and of his responsibility to the colony, he just laughed. He said getting the uranium meant more to him than anything in the world." The little professor sighed. "If it hadn't been for the cadets, he would have gotten away with it."

"But wait a minute," said Roger. "If you suspected Vidac, why did you give him the information on the uranium to send back to the Solar Guard?"

"I just told him about a puny little deposit near the Logan farm," replied Sykes. "The big strike is on the other side of the satellite. I figured that if Vidac was honest it wouldn't hurt to delay sending information back about the big strike until later." He paused and added, "But then, of course, I had to tell him about the big strike."

"You had to tell him!" exclaimed Jeff. "But why?"

"To stay alive, you idiot!" barked Sykes. "As long as I had something they wanted, they'd keep me alive until they found out about it. They gave me truth serum, but I'm immune to drugs. All Solar Guard scientists are. They didn't know that. So I told them to look here, then there, acted as though I had lost my memory. It worked, and here I am."

"What about the way they antagonized us?" asked Tom. "Refusing to let us contact Space Academy and sending us out on a stripped-down rocket scout to investigate the asteroid cluster. It seems to me they should have acted a little more friendly to throw us off the track. All they did was arouse suspicion and get us sore."

"But they hoped that you would get angry enough to do something rebellious, so that they could send you back," said Sykes.

"Well, that makes sense," said Strong. "But what about their treatment of the colonists?"

"Humph. A clear case of attempting to get the colonists to rebel which would give them the right to absolute control of the entire satellite and the people. Cadet Tom Corbett here is to be congratulated for not allowing Mr. Logan to go around like a vigilante and get us all in a space hurricane!"

Hyram Logan blushed and cleared his throat noisily.

The door suddenly opened and a uniformed messenger thrust a dispatch into Strong's hands.

"What's this?" asked Strong, tearing the Solar Guard seal.

"Message from spaceport control, sir," said the messenger. "They report a fleet of ships approaching Roald, under full thrust."

"A fleet!" gasped Strong. "But how? Why?"

Sykes laughed, winked at Jane, and slapped his thigh. "The Solar Guard coming to the rescue!"

"Solar Guard!" chorused the others at the table.

"Yes! Solar Guard. I sent for them. I figured if the cadets could build a communicator, I could too. I did it on the *Polaris* when Hardy went searching for the uranium. I told the whole story to Commander Walters back at Space Academy."

"Well," sighed Roger, "with the confession Jeff got from Winters on the audioscriber, I guess we can consider the first civil disorder of the star satellite of Roald finished. Peace and harmony will reign. And speaking of harmony, Jane, would you like to take a walk in the starlight?"

"I'm sorry, Roger," answered Jane, blushing prettily, "but I've already been invited."

Roger's face fell. "You've already been invited?"

Jane nodded. "Ready, Astro?"

"Sure!" replied the giant Venusian. He rose, offered Jane his arm ceremoniously, and the two walked out of the house. Roger's face turned a deep scarlet. The others around the table burst into laughter.

"Ah, go blow your jets," growled Roger.

Billy's eyes were shining. He turned to Strong. "Captain Strong, how old do you have to be to get into Space Academy?"

Strong's eyes twinkled. "Since Roger doesn't seem to be too busy, why don't you ask him for all the Academy dope?"

"Would you help me, Roger?" pleaded Billy. "I can recite the whole book of Academy 'regs' by heart!"

Roger glanced around the table with a sheepish grin. "There isn't but one regulation that's really important, Billy."

"Oh? What's that?"

"I'll answer that, Billy," said Tom. "Roger means the one that goes like this . . . 'no cadet will be allowed to entertain any work, project, or ideas that will not lend themselves directly to his immediate or future obligation as a spaceman.'" Tom stopped and smiled broadly. "And that means girls!"

BIBLIOBAZAAR

The essential book market!

Did you know that you can get any of our titles in large print?

Did you know that we have an ever-growing collection of books in many languages?

Order online:
www.bibliobazaar.com

Find all of your favorite classic books!

Stay up to date with the latest government reports!

At BiblioBazaar, we aim to make knowledge more accessible by making thousands of titles available to you- *quickly and affordably*.

Contact us:
BiblioBazaar
PO Box 21206
Charleston, SC 29413

Amazon Marketplace (The Book Depository) Mar 2010